ACT OF GOD

DEFIANCE #3

JASON KRUMBINE

Published by Lantern Key Books

ISBN: 978-1-971197-02-9

Originally published in 2019 by Jason Krumbine

First Lantern Key Books Edition: December 2025

about this book

In this explosive follow up to the Hand of God, the crew of the USS Defiance find themselves on the edge of UPA space, cut off from any assistance, floating helplessly among the stars.

Across the ship, systems are failing.

Repairs could take days, maybe even weeks, but with limited life support, the crew only has hours.

While the ship threatens to come apart around them, Lt. Commander Nax is slowly going mad, haunted by the ghost of his dead lover.

Tactical Officer Cayden Keane lies in critical condition, barely clinging to life after suffering at the hands of the Unity.

Trapped in what appears to be a no-win scenario, the crew of the Defiance turns to their captain.

Except Captain Gavin Mitchell is missing.

He's not on the ship.

He's not in their sector.

Gavin Mitchell isn't even in their universe anymore.

Books in the Defiance Series

Defiance
Hand of God
Act of God
The Test of Truth
The Price of Paradise
The Value of Terror
The Last Breath of a Dying Tomorrow

Subscribe to my newsletter and I'll let you know as soon as the next Defiance book is ready to read.

https://onestrayword.beehiiv.com/subscribe

ACT OF GOD

previously...

Dispatched to investigate a mysterious SOS signal transmitted in a code that hadn't been used in hundreds of years the Defiance stumbles across a vessel from another universe entirely.

After Captain Mitchell dispatches a boarding party to investigate, he's visited by an all-powerful entity named Steve.

According to Steve, their universe is simply one of many, stacked atop one other. Steve is from the top of the Stack. The Unity is from the bottom and it's slowly working its way up, consuming every universe in its path. He warns Mitchell to bring the boarding party back before it's too late.

The boarding party is made up of Lt. Commander Nax, Doctor Dheer, Lt. Commander Keane and Chief Engineer Warrick.

Unbeknownst to the rest of the crew, Nax has been unable to sleep since the death of his lover, Grace Hawkins, the former first officer of the Defiance. He finds himself haunted by what appears to be her ghost.

Dheer and Keane discover a member of the Unity imprisoned on the ship. According to the ship's logs, this member of the Unity seems to be unwell, which is what allowed them to capture it in the first place.

In an attempt to restore main power to the vessel, Warrick and his people set off some kind of self-destruct protocol that not only results in a meltdown of the main power core but also releases the Unity. Once free, the Unity attacks, nearly killing Keane.

With the ship about to explode, Mitchell implores Steve to save his crew. Frustrated with the fact that Mitchell doesn't seem to be listening, Steve does bring the boarding party back. However, the Defiance is too close to the vessel as it begins to explode and cannot get away in time.

As soon as the boarding party returns, Steve disappears taking Mitchell with him and leaving the Defiance to their own fate.

1

SOMEPLACE ELSE

A LONG TIME AGO

THE MAN STOOD in front of the door. He was overwhelmed with anticipation, his body practically vibrating.

All the systems flashed green.

And yet…

The man did not reach for the door.

His hands did not move to grasp the handle of the door.

Why?

He stared down at his hands with an alien expression. These were his hands, yes? The same hands he had been born with? They must be, he concluded. If no other reason, he could not recall a time when his hands were replaced.

But if they were his hands, why did they not *feel* like his hands? Why did they not *look* like his hands?

The man looked up at the door again.

Of course.

Perception was *everything*.

And *everything* was about to change.

Once he opened that door, he would no longer be the

same man he was. His hands would no longer be the same hands he had been born with.

Reality itself would no longer be the same.

He held his hands in front of his face and chuckled.

Perception was everything.

Of course they were *his* hands.

He turned his hands around to look at their backs. Yes, they were most definitely his hands.

He had known they were his hands all along, of course. They hadn't changed. They *couldn't* change.

No. He was the one who was changing and that was okay.

He wasn't particularly fond of the man he was.

They laughed at that man. They mocked him. They called him a fool. And then they had laughed at him again.

They had all laughed so much at him.

So, no, he wasn't going to miss that version of himself.

Because now he was going to become the man who changed everything.

He lowered his hands and took a deep breath, closing his eyes to savor the moment.

Everything.

Behind him something beeped. An alert. On this side of the door time was infinite.

On the other side of the door, however, time was not.

It beeped again, reminding the man of this.

He exhaled slowly and opened his eyes.

Yes, of course, *time*.

He glanced up at the glass covered observation deck.

It was empty, as he knew it would be.

Despite how they mocked him endlessly, he had invited them all.

And why not? This was history in the making. Had they all become so jaded that they couldn't see that?

He shook his head.

Of course they had.

He knew they weren't going to come. He hoped they would have. But he knew such hope was in vain.

And yet, *hope* was what brought him to this moment today.

He couldn't help himself.

Behind him the alert beeped again. He imagined it sounded almost impatient this time. *Time*, it reminded him, *was running out.* If he did not open the door soon, he would not have another opportunity to do so for a very, very, very long time.

But, of course, time was *relative*.

But even he didn't want to have to wait that *long*.

But, the man decided he could wait just a little bit longer.

He glanced back at the observation deck once more. They wouldn't all come, of course. But, maybe, just maybe, *she* might?

Certainly he could wait for her.

As if in response, the alert beeped again, nagging him. *No*, it insisted, *he really couldn't wait for her. History waited for no one.*

The man turned back to the door.

History waited for no one.

Except in the past where it waited for everyone.

The man steeled himself.

He shook off his insecurities, his doubts, his fears and his loneliness. He tossed them aside as easily as he tossed aside the man he *was* for the man he was going to *become*.

He took a step forward, reaching for the door.

His hand brushed across the polished chrome of the handle and a chill ran down his spine. *Anticipation*, he told himself.

His calculations were *sound*.

His theories were about to become *fact*.

"This is going to work," he whispered and before his doubts could get another word in, he grabbed the handle of the door and flung it open.

The *abyss*.

The end of everything.

The beginning of everything.

The man stared into the yawning abyss, looking for an end to it, but instead found himself growing dizzy by the sight. Of course there was no end. The abyss simply *was*.

The man nearly giggled.

It was exactly as he imagined it would be.

He took a moment and tore his gaze away from the open doorway to double check the readings. Everything remained green. The singularity fields were holding.

Of course they were.

Because he was *right*.

Everything was going to be different now.

Everything.

He turned back to the door and took it all in.

The darkness on the other side stretched out for eternity.

This was the very end of reality.

This was the beginning of reality.

This was what they had mocked him for seeking and here that would end as it would lead to a new beginning.

His mind raced with the possibilities.

The discoveries.

The Laws of Reality were going to be rewritten and he was going to have the honor of authoring them himself.

Absently he noticed his cheeks were wet.

His fingers brushed across the moisture tentatively, as if

coming into contact with an alien substance. He almost laughed when he realized what it was.

He was *crying*.

Of course he was.

This was his life's work.

Everything had led to this moment. And it was...

Something shifted in the darkness.

His eyes tried to pin it down, but it was impossible to separate the darkness from itself.

The man blinked. His eyes must have deceived him. There was nothing there.

He rubbed his eyes.

The darkness moved again, swirling around itself. It moved as though it was both separate from itself and wholly part of itself all at once.

This was not possible, he knew.

Behind him there was a new alert. A harsher sound. A screeching alarm. But it seemed distant to him, as though coming from the other side of creation.

There was something in the darkness. What was it?

The new alarm grew fainter as he leaned forward, anxious to see a thing that should not, could not, exist here in the abyss of reality.

The darkness surged forward towards him.

The man realized his mistake. The distant alarm suddenly coming back to him.

But by then, it was much too late.

The darkness reached for him, wrapping itself around him and pulling him in. It pierced his skin, digging into his very essence. Unimaginable pain exploded across his body.

He struggled in vain against it. He opened his mouth to shout an alarm, someone needed to know what was out there, and the darkness poured down his throat before a single sound could escape him.

The man could feel the darkness consuming him, digesting bits and pieces of his body, his mind, his *identity*.

Fresh tears streamed down his face. They were quickly consumed by the darkness.

There was a spark as the darkness yanked him through the singularity field.

A new alarm sounded and the door to the abyss slammed closed.

2

STARBASE ATLANTIC

NOW

MUCH TO HER SURPRISE, Commodore Kathryn Straub found herself deeply engrossed in a torrid romance.

To anybody who might pop into her office, it would appear that she was simply reviewing the day's reports with rapt enthusiasm. A reasonable assumption to make, considering that she was, after all, on duty.

But daily reports did not have the seductive sizzle that Straub found herself currently engrossed in.

It was not, traditionally, considered good form to be reading for pleasure while on duty. And reading the type of romance novel as she was, even less so.

But her job came with a certain amount of…stress.

Usually, Straub dealt with this stress by simply chewing out her subordinates in such a manner that would leave nearly anyone a weeping puddle in a darkened corner.

It had recently been suggested, after breaking one particular new ensign, Straub might want to consider another form of stress relief.

So she decided to start reading romance novels while on duty.

On the surface, it didn't seem to be a particularly inventive solution.

However, she quickly found that the romance novels afforded her an immediate disconnect from the stress-ridden environment around her.

Of course, she also soon discovered they created another problem that she had difficulty dealing with as well. But she decided it was still probably better than emotionally and mentally tearing down her subordinates.

Somebody cleared their throat and Straub looked up, surprised and startled.

Lieutenant Commander Mallozzi stood awkwardly in the doorway. His long arms were clasped behind his back and his narrow eyes seemed even more narrow as they squinted at her.

"I knocked," Mallozzi said.

Straub took a long moment, mentally running back the last minute. Exactly how engrossed had she been in her book?

"You didn't answer," Mallozzi added.

"Of course." Upon realizing that sounded unusually high-pitched, Straub cleared her throat and set the datapad on her desk, screen down.

Mallozzi eyed the datapad suspiciously. That wasn't the usual response for showing up unannounced in the Commodore's office. "Is everything okay?"

Straub rubbed at her throat, avoiding his eyes for a second. "Fine. Everything's fine."

"Fine?"

"*Fine.*"

Something that passed for bemusement appeared on Mallozzi's face. "You don't sound particularly fine."

"It could be because my third shift commander just popped into my office unannounced," Straub said.

"I'm not exactly a stealthy creature," Mallozzi said. "There's a good reason why there's never been an Aztix in covert ops."

"So I've been told," Straub said diplomatically.

"I'm just saying, I'm not known for quietly entering a room."

"There's several things you're not known for doing quietly," Straub said. "I've lost count of the number of times I've had to speak with you about your bathing routine."

"Well, you could always move my quarters down to C deck," he suggested.

"That'd probably get me into more trouble with the Fleet's diversity team," Straub replied. "I don't want to have to explain why I moved my Aztix officer next door to the trash recyclers."

Mallozzi shrugged his slender shoulders. "Personally, I would find the smell far preferable to what I normally have to put up with from my fellow officers."

Straub sighed, rubbing her tired forehead. "Is there a legitimate reason you're here? Or is this just another roundabout way to argue your case for moving your quarters again?"

Mallozzi glanced at the datapad. "I'm not interrupting something, am I?"

"Of course you're interrupting something," Straub said. "You're always interrupting something. You live to interrupt things."

"I don't know that I would go that far," Mallozzi said. "Although, I won't deny I do get a little thrill every time I interrupt Ambassador Reynoso at the Daboo tables. It almost always costs him a small fortune in credits and self-esteem."

She shook her head. "Are you here to nag me some

more about Ogletree? Because not only have I already apologized to him, I wrote him a recommendation that he would most likely never deserve. Hell, I've got two medals of honor and *I* wouldn't deserve it."

Mallozzi raised both of his eyebrows. "I did not expect that."

"What? I've been known to have a way with the written word."

"No, you remembered his name. Also, the letter of recommendation is a nice touch," he said. "I'm not sure how it'll heal the emotional scars of you tearing off strips of his soul, but maybe he can print it out and hang it on his wall. You know, as something to look upon whenever he wakes up in the middle of the night, covered in a cold sweat."

"Marv…"

"I've been reviewing that signal from the Uslen system."

Straub looked at him, confused. "The Morse code signal?"

He nodded. "It…bothered me."

"The *Defiance* is already investigating it," Straub said. "Last report I got from Mitchell said he was sending an away team over to the ship. I don't think the signal's going to end up being anything important. It looks like it's a dead ship."

"That's not what's bothering me." Mallozzi stepped up to the desk and called up a holographic schematic Straub wasn't familiar with. "It's the amount of data in the signal that the computer couldn't decipher. The S.O.S. segment was relatively small in comparison to the signal as a whole. The computer estimates there could be almost eighty petabytes of data in the signal."

"But it's not in any form that we recognize," Straub said.

Mallozzi nodded. "That's what bothered me. Somebody went to a lot of trouble to encode all this data into the transmission. Why put it in a format we couldn't read?"

Straub frowned. "Is this going to turn into some kind of philosophical debate on how different species should all follow the same pattern of logic-based thinking?"

"Not at all," Mallozzi replied. "I'm simply building up to this." He adjusted the image, turning it sideways and then expanding it into four different layers. "The Uboklu have a system of data management that involves encoding information through auditory signals. It's not a particularly popular method of data management among the majority of the UPA, considering that Uboklu are the only species in the UPA who have auditory systems hyper-developed enough to detect the data shifts. But it's a thing that exists. It occurred to me that perhaps we were looking at a thing that we should have been listening to. Once I reset the computer's parameters on how to examine the signal, this is what I got."

Straub leaned forward and tilted her head to the side to get a closer look, studying dots that spread out in a haphazard manner, connected by jagged lines. "So what is it?"

"What does it look like?"

Straub shot him a look. "It looks like an art project from a six-year-old Fe'ihrek."

Mallozzi frowned. "We both know that's not true. Most Fe'ihrek can barely speak, let alone comprehend the nature of art, before their thirty-fifth year."

Straub sighed. "You're an asshole, Marv."

He shrugged his slender shoulders. "Perhaps. Despite

your threats, you haven't bumped me down to space janitor yet, though."

Straub studied the image for another moment. "Alright." She folded her arms. "It looks like, a map?"

Mallozzi nodded. "That's my conclusion as well."

"Great," Straub said. "We both think it looks like a map. You have any idea what it's a map of? Because otherwise, it's not going to be a very useful map."

Mallozzi called up a new image, superimposing it over the map. "As I'm sure you recognize, this is a star chart of sectors forty-nine through fifty-three." He gestured to a spot highlighted on both the star chart and the map from the signal. "This is where the *Defiance* reported the wormhole in the Neutral Zone. And this," he pointed to another spot that appeared on both charts, "is where we logged the wormhole in the Uslen system. By that logic, I don't think it's wrong to assume that the rest of these," Mallozzi waved a hand and both the map and the star chart expanded to include over half of the UPA where dozens of locations were highlighted across the maps, "are also points where wormholes may be located. Kathryn, I think somebody on that ship figured out how to map this wormhole network and was very desperate to make sure they weren't the only ones to use it."

3

USS DEFIANCE

THERE WAS DARKNESS AND SILENCE.

Then Sadie Sadler woke up.

She regained consciousness with a start, almost jolting upright, as though an electrical current was suddenly running through her body.

Surrounded by dim red emergency lights and dull, squawking alarms, for a moment she couldn't remember where she was or what had happened.

All she knew was that everything *hurt*.

Sadler was on the floor. Something at the back of her head stung especially bad. She reached back with her fingers to inspect it and winced as she touched the injured area. Nothing felt wet and when she examined her fingers in the dim light, they weren't covered in blood, but instead thick scorch marks. It didn't surprise her. While Sadler was human, she grew up on Thyor and as such, her skin, like most humans raised under Thyor's unique atmospheric properties was difficult to pierce.

She reached up with her other hand, grabbing the edge of her console and pulled herself up from the floor of the bridge, coughing as she inhaled the thick smoke that billowed out from the exposed ceiling panels.

Sparks exploded from her station, causing her to jump back and it all came flooding back to her.

The ship was in *danger*.

There had been another ship. An older ship, from another universe?

Sadler squeezed her eyes shut. The stinging at the back of her head jolted across to her forehead. She pressed the palms of her hands against her temples and took a deep breath, trying to focus.

The main core of the other ship had reached critical mass and the *Defiance* was too close. The resultant explosion threatened to destroy the *Defiance* as well.

The captain had…

Done nothing.

He had done nothing.

Why had Captain Mitchell done nothing?

Sadler blinked and looked around the bridge, straining to see through the thick smoke.

Her gaze fell upon Keane's bloody body, his left arm missing, and the rest of her memory resolved itself.

Captain Mitchell was gone.

Taken by some extra-dimensional being.

Where the hell had he taken Captain Mitchell?

Around the bridge, officers were getting to their feet.

Fans kicked in and the smoke started to clear.

The captain was gone and there was no first officer.

No captain.

No first officer.

The next in command was…

Her.

"Shit."

4

SADLER STUMBLED OVER TO KEANE, kneeling down next to him, intent on checking to see if he was still alive.

But before she could look for a pulse, he jolted suddenly, coughing up blood.

Then a hand grabbed her wrist, stopping her from getting any closer.

It was Dheer. The side of her face was streaked with blood. "Don't touch him." She looked at Keane's leg. There was a dark, oily substance leaking from just above his knee. It stood out sharply against his ashen skin.

Sadler pulled her hand back. "You're hurt," she said to Dheer.

Dheer brushed her off. "It's a scratch."

Sadler wasn't going to argue the point. She nodded at Keane. "What's wrong with him?"

"Other than the fact he's dying?" Dheer grunted, pulling her dark hair back from her face.

"Yeah, okay," Sadler said. "Other than that?"

Dheer wiped the blood from the side of her face. She

didn't bother to answer Sadler. "I need to get him down to the surgical bay immediately."

Sadler looked around the bridge. The lighting was dim, nothing more than a faint red glow from the emergency power lights. The dull, squawking alarm was still going off. It grated against her ears and she realized that she actually flinched every time it blared over the speakers. She wasn't entirely certain, but it felt as though the ship was almost tilting.

Sadler looked back at Keane. He looked like a corpse. She didn't know what to say, so she didn't bother saying anything at all.

Sadler started to get back to her feet when Dheer grabbed her arm again. "If I can't get him into the surgical bay soon, he *will* die. He's already lost too much blood."

"I don't know what to tell you, doc. For all I know we've got a hull breach somewhere and we're all about to end up dead anyway" Sadler said and made her way to the command chair.

"Aren't you supposed to be the optimistic one?" Dheer asked her.

"I like to shake it up every once in a while." Sadler dropped herself into the command chair. It felt wrong. She thought that maybe from the command chair, she might feel like she was in charge. But instead she simply felt like she was keeping the seat warm for the captain, as usual. But there was nothing usual about any of this.

The main viewscreen was blank. Moments ago the *Eternal Hand of God* had been up there, breaking up. Now they didn't even have a view of the stars.

Sadler clutched at the armrests of the command chair. She needed to stay focused. She took a deep breath and said the first thing that she thought made sense, "Anybody around here want to let me know what the hell happened?"

No one replied.

What the hell was she supposed to do with that?

There was a loud groan from the far end of the bridge and a figure with bright white hair slowly got to his feet. "Feels like every damn bone in my body is broken," Rabkin said, holding his hand against the wall for support. "Is it my imagination or is the damn ship tilting?"

"Jury's still out on it," Sadler said.

Rabkin looked around. "What the hell happened?"

Sadler held up her hands. "I'm still trying to figure that one out."

There was a grunt from the direction of the helm and an orange figure slowly got to his feet. Nax.

A second later, a shorter, bald figure with a thick, bushy beard pulled himself up from the other side of the helm.

"Warrick," Sadler practically breathed a sigh of relief. "What the hell is going on?"

Warrick groaned and carefully pulled a shard of glass from his arm. "How the hell should I know? A minute ago I was trapped on a gorram ghost ship that was about to go critical with no flarkin' way to get off it. Next thing I know I'm here watching the captain disappear into thin air."

"Right. Right." Sadler fumbled with the comm, briefly forgetting which channel engineering was on. "Bridge to engineering."

There was no answer. Just static.

"That's not encouraging," Rabkin said, moving around the bridge as he checked the other crewmen.

Nax settled in at the helm and attempted to access his screens. "It would appear that main power is currently down."

"Wonderful," Sadler said.

Rabkin knelt down next to Dheer. He checked the cut on her forehead. "Main power's down but we've still got enough juice for that damn alarm to go off?"

As if in response, the dull, squawking alarm seemed to raise its volume.

"Son of a bitch," Sadler muttered.

Nax held up a finger and then made an adjustment on his console. The alarm immediately went silent.

Sadler breathed a sigh of relief. "Thank you." She took a breath and exhaled. "What alarm was that for anyway?"

Warrick made a face. "Hull breach."

"Son of a bitch," Sadler repeated. "How bad?"

Warrick looked over Nax's shoulder and made a few adjustments. "I can't tell from here. It can't be too bad, though. Life support seems to be holding."

"That's good?" Sadler asked.

"It's not something I could trade for a night with a six-breasted Faulir."

Sadler slowly spun around in the command chair, running her hands over her face. She tried to take stock of everything that had happened, but she was having difficulty getting a handle on a situation that seemed to be getting worse at every turn.

"I don't mean to nag," Rabkin said, kneeling next to Keane. "But we really need to get Keane down to sickbay."

Sadler looked at him and then at Keane. "Right. Keane." She turned back to Warrick. "Tell me the lifts are at least working."

Warrick tapped something on the console and then glanced back at the lift at the rear of the bridge. The door slid open with a heavy scratching noise.

"That's at least something." Sadler looked around the bridge again and hesitated. She felt like she should probably say something. But what was she going to say? Half the bridge looked just as dazed she felt.

Rabkin muttered something under his breath and got back to his feet. He gestured to two crewmen who didn't seem to have more than a few scratches. "You two, congratulations. You just got promoted as my new orderlies. Now get the hell over here and do exactly as I say."

"Okay." Sadler nodded and tried not to feel like a kid who just got chastised by her grandfather. She turned back to Warrick and Nax.

"I need to get down to engineering," Warrick said. "I can't do anything from here."

Sadler nodded. "Right. Do that. Get the comms back up as quickly as you can."

Warrick nodded and headed for the lift.

Sadler didn't move from the command chair. She stared at the blank viewscreen.

"Commander?" Nax said after a moment. When she didn't respond, he said, "Sadie?"

Sadler blinked and looked at him. "I'm sorry. I just…" She shook her head as if to clear out her fuzzy thoughts. "Never mind. What is it?"

"What happened to Captain Mitchell?" Nax asked.

Sadler remembered the captain disappearing into thin air with Steve. She shook her head. "I honestly have no idea."

5

"I'll tell you what happened to the captain," Grace Hawkins said. She raised an inviting eyebrow as she spoke.

Nax struggled to maintain his composure. He turned away from Sadler and back towards the helm as naturally as he could.

"What's the matter?" Hawkins asked him. She stood to his left on the other side of the helm. As he turned, she casually walked around until she was in front of him again.

Nax kept his focus on his console. His heart pounded away in his chest rapidly. Despite the fact that he did not possess any sweat glands, the palms of his hands felt clammy. He reached for his console, unsure of what to do.

Hawkins had appeared almost immediately.

There was a brief moment when he lost consciousness in the aftermath of the explosive shockwave hitting the *Defiance*. He had dropped to the ground, banging his head against the flat surface of the helm and blacked out.

When he came to, she had been standing over him.

Commander Grace Hawkins.

No one else seemed to notice her and why should they? After all, she was *dead*.

And yet, there she was, standing between him and the viewscreen. She leaned across the helm and waved a hand in his face.

"Hello? Anybody home?" she asked him.

It took considerable effort not to reply.

When she was alive, they had been lovers.

And in death, he had come to realize they had been much more than that.

And so it took every ounce of strength he possessed to not reply to her.

She rested her chin on the back of her hands. "I know you're a man of few words, but this is ridiculous."

There was something in the tone of her voice. Something…familiar and it touched a part of Nax that he wasn't comfortable with

For a brief second, he glanced up at her.

Hawkins smiled at him.

She looked exactly as she had when she had been alive. Tall, almost statuesque, with a light complexion and soft features that were quick to harden when she was on duty. The former first officer of the *Defiance* didn't command respect or attention. She simply had a natural charisma that people instantly connected with. She had been an excellent first officer.

She had been an even better lover.

Nax made a strangled noise at the back of his throat. He hesitated, certain somebody would have heard him and would express either concern or interest in him. He found himself suddenly nervous and unsettled at the prospect of Sadler asking if everything was okay.

Because, of course, nothing was okay.

His dead lover was talking to him.

There was not a single civilization in the galaxy where that was considered 'okay.'

But Sadler didn't say anything. Neither did anyone else.

Nax exhaled a breath he hadn't been aware he had been holding.

"You need to relax," Hawkins said. "You're too high strung. I know, given the situation that seems like, well, a stupid thing to say. But people are *counting* on you. Relying on you. And you can't do your job if you're emotionally strung out. So, you need to relax. You're out of danger, for now at least. The ship isn't going to suddenly blow up." She paused and then added, "At least, I hope it's not. So, relax. Take a deep breath and just, *relax*. You're still alive and that has to count for something, right?"

Nax didn't reply.

He *wouldn't* reply.

Grace Hawkins was dead and what was standing in front of him right now was simply a figment of his imagination.

And if he started talking to figments of his imagination, then Nax had problems far greater than he should have.

"Are you sure about that?" Hawkins asked him, as though she had been reading his mind.

Despite himself, Nax glanced up at her again.

"Are you sure I'm just part of your imagination?" she asked. "As I recall, and granted my memory's not always been the best. But, wasn't I the...*imaginative* one?" She smiled suggestively at him.

And suddenly, Nax felt an odd pang in his chest.

For a moment he thought there was something wrong with him and then he recognized it for what it was: emotion.

And not for the first time since she had passed, Nax wished he could cry.

6

    ————

"Nax? *Nax?*"

Nax jerked upright and spun around abruptly to face Sadler. She was staring at him with a look on her face which suggested he had missed something important she had said.

He turned to look where Hawkins had been a moment ago, but the space was empty. There was no indication of his dead lover anywhere.

"Nax?" Sadler asked again. "Are you with us?"

Using every ounce of his willpower, Nax managed to not break down right then and there. He cleared his throat. "Sorry, Commander. I was…lost in thought."

His eyes flicked around the helm, looking for any sign of Hawkins' presence. But there was none. Because, of course, she was dead, and he was far sicker than he was willing to admit to even himself.

Sadler got up from the command chair and stepped over to the helm. A look of concern passed over her face. She lowered her voice. "Now's not a great time if you're planning on launching into another ancient Natuzzi grieving ritual."

Nax looked directly into Sadler's eyes and did everything in his willpower to appear perfectly normal. "I can assure you, that is not going to happen."

Sadler paused, studying his face. There were twitches at the corners of his eyes that betrayed him. "Are you okay?"

"I am…" Nax trailed off for a moment. He took a deep breath and finally said, "Fine." Despite himself, there was a faint sound of strain in his voice.

"Fine?" Sadler echoed.

"Fine," Nax repeated more forcefully.

Sadler looked around the bridge, but no one seemed to be paying them any attention. "Fine is not exactly how I would describe your demeanor right now." She held up a finger. "This is you." With her other hand she gestured towards the debris on the viewscreen. "*Fine* is somewhere out there, amid the wreckage of a ship from another damn universe."

Nax closed his eyes and pinched the bridge of his nose as he took a deep breath. He looked at her with as much sincerity as he could muster. "It has been a…*difficult* day."

"Difficult?" Sadler snorted. "Yeah, no shit." When Nax didn't seem inclined to offer anything more, she exhaled and said, "Look, Nax, I understand you're still dealing with your loss of Hawkins and it is affecting you in ways that maybe I can't understand. And, in addition, hell, maybe you need some time to, I don't know, absorb what happened to you on that ship and get caught up to speed on what's been going on over here, but that's time I can't give you right now."

"I completely understand," Nax replied, his voice sounding surprisingly even.

"Do you? Because I sure as hell don't," Sadler said. "The captain is *gone*, Nax. Hawkins is *gone*. It's just *me* now." She held up both hands, palms out. "And that's not great. I'm not the kind of command figure you want in a situation like this. I'm the kind of commander you need when things are really boring and uneventful. When the shit hits the fan? You don't call me." She paused and took a deep breath. "What I'm saying is, I need you *here* right now." She reached over and tapped on the console. "*Here.*"

Nax cleared his throat again. He forced his hands to unclench from the armrest of his chair. "I completely understand," he repeated. "This situation has my complete, undivided attention."

Sadler chewed on her lower lip, watching him and looking entirely unconvinced. "Right. You realize how unconvincing that sounds?"

Nax nodded. "Yes, I do. Unfortunately, I don't have anything else to offer you right now."

"So I'm just supposed to take you at your word that you're not going to flip out on me?"

"The alternative is that you have me confined to quarters," Nax said. "But that seems like an unreasonable use of resources."

Sadler sighed. "Right. Sure. Unreasonable use of resources. That sounds like a thing."

"The captain is missing," Nax said after a few seconds of silence.

Sadler ran a hand through her short blond hair. "Yeah, best case scenario."

"Worst case?"

"Well, when the same entity took Zemble, he ended up in some kind of dimension where he couldn't breathe and apparently lost all sense of time. I'll be the first to admit that the captain's one of the most strong-willed people I know, but I can't imagine a scenario where he doesn't end up dead if he can't breathe."

Nax arched a hairless eyebrow and tilted his head to the side. "That seems like a fair assessment."

Sadler rubbed the side of her face and pointed to the empty viewscreen. "The *Eternal Hand of God* reached critical mass. When it went, we were too close to survive. We shouldn't even be here having this conversation. Trust me on this, I was paying *very* close attention to those readings. And even if we were able to engage the ion drive at the last second, we would have still been caught by a shockwave that should have ripped out our hull."

"That is interesting," Nax murmured and slowly turned back to his console.

"Sure." Sadler's headed bobbed. "That's one way of putting it."

Nax ignored her as he worked his console. "According to our sensors, we haven't moved."

Sadler shook her head, chewing on her thumbnail.

"Logs show that the helm was primed, but the engines were never engaged," Nax continued.

"Then, quite frankly, we should all be dead," Sadler said. "And I'm pretty sure none of us are dead right now. Because despite any reservations I have about a higher power governing our universe, I'm pretty damn sure that the afterlife isn't just a continuation of our regular life."

"I am certainly inclined to agree," Nax replied. "The sensors logged some kind of energy eruption?"

"It's called the ship blowing up, Nax," Sadler said.

"Not when it's seconds before the actual explosion," Nax replied evenly.

Sadler moved closer, looking over his shoulder. "What?"

Nax gestured to the data. "According to the sensors, the

energy eruption acted as some kind of shield against the bulk of the explosion, absorbing almost," he paused, double checking the readings, "nearly eighty percent of the blast."

Sadler looked up at the viewscreen. Debris from the ship floated in space around them. "That wasn't our shields."

Nax shook his head. "It's point of origin was just off our forward bow."

"And even if it had been our shields," Sadler said. "At a hundred percent, I'm not entirely certain they would have been able to absorb that much of the blast. Put it up on the screen."

The viewscreen switched from the debris to an empty section of space approximately six miles off their forward bow.

Sadler stared blankly at the screen for several seconds before finally saying, "There's nothing there."

Nax looked up from his console, his face a mask of mild surprise. "And according to our sensors, there never was."

"So where the hell did that energy shield come from?"

7

"WHAT THE HELL do you think you're doing?" Rabkin asked Dheer.

Sickbay was crowded with injured crewmen. It was already a small space, built to only handle five or six patients at a time. Now, however, beds were occupied with multiple patients and crewmen who didn't have a place to sit, leaned against each other, propping each other up.

Dheer shoved past them all, racing as quickly as she could for the surgical suite. "I need to get prepped."

"For what?" Rabkin snapped.

"Surgery," Dheer snapped back.

Rabkin grabbed her shoulder, pulling her to a stop just outside the surgical suite. "Are you out of your damn mind."

She pushed his hand off. "I have a patient who's *dying*."

"Are you eager to help him shuffle off faster?" Rabkin said.

Dheer jerked back as though she had been slapped. "What the hell is that supposed to mean?"

"It means that if you think I'm letting you operate on

Keane you are most definitely out of your damn mind." Rabkin caught the eye of one of the nurses attending to a crewman with a broken arm. "Prep for surgery. Keane's on the table."

"Hey, I'm not arguing with you about this," Dheer snapped.

"Good," Rabkin said, pushing past her. "Saves me time that's better spent on saving Keane's life."

"Hey," Dheer started, but Rabkin cut her off.

"In case you've forgotten, I still outrank you," he said. "So right there, that means I don't have to explain myself to you. I give you an order and you snap-to. That's how this is supposed to work."

Dheer glared at him, not trusting herself to say anything.

"But by taking the time to have this conversation," Rabkin continued, "I hope you can appreciate how much I respect you. Because if I didn't, I wouldn't be bothering with this right now."

"Listen-" she started again, and Rabkin cut her off with a wave of his hand.

"I don't know what the hell happened over on that damn ship, but it doesn't take a rocket scientist to recognize that shit hit the fan," he said. "You're in no position to be cutting open anybody right now. Hell, right now, the best thing you can do is find a damn corner to curl up in and take five minutes to freak out."

Dheer jabbed her finger at him and before she could say anything, Rabkin simply nodded at her hand. It was trembling.

Her other hand came up, clasping itself over her trembling hand, pulling it back down.

"I trust I made my point?" Rabkin asked.

Dheer sucked in an unsteady breath. "You're right."

"Of course I'm right," Rabkin said. "I'm always right. It's a blessing and a curse." He turned back to the surgical suite. He scanned Keane's vitals on a nearby screen. They were weak. In addition to the arm, he had lost almost six pints of blood. And then there was his leg. The computer didn't know what to make of it. It had some kind of foreign mass that seemed to be infecting him. "What the hell happened over there? I don't need the whole damn story, just the highlights."

Dheer pressed a hand to the side of her head. Suddenly she was feeling lightheaded and almost woozy as the rush of adrenaline began to wear off. "We were attacked."

"No shit," Rabkin grumbled.

"By the Unity," Dheer finished.

Rabkin glanced back at her, both of his bushy eyebrows went up. "No shit?"

Dheer cupped her hands over her mouth as her whole body shuddered. "I...don't know. I don't know. It wasn't like on Carlock. It was different. It was *worse*. It was..." She looked past Rabkin at Keane's unconscious body. "He shouldn't have been there and if he hadn't, I'd be dead right now."

8

ERIN CALLOWAY WAS certain she was going mad.

In the confusing aftermath she ducked off the bridge behind Rabkin and Dheer. No one noticed her. Their focus, rightly so, was on Keane.

Keane...

Before Calloway had stepped foot on the *Defiance* she had seen exactly two dead bodies. Her grandparents on her mother's side. Both had passed away peacefully in their sleep after nearly sixty years together.

Now, though, it felt like all she saw was dead bodies.

After everybody left the lift she stayed, huddled at the back wall as if she was going to turn invisible.

Something wasn't...right.

She felt *wrong*.

But she didn't know what was wrong.

It was like there was another voice in her head, speaking to her. Or maybe speaking *with* her? But she couldn't hear it. She strained to hear it, but it kept getting farther away, without moving at all.

Yes, she was fairly certain she was going mad.

Since the encounter on Carlock, Calloway had been having difficulty with sleep. Every time she attempted to close her eyes and give her body the rest it desperately needed; she would hear that *voice*.

That muffled, distant voice.

What was it saying? Was it saying anything? Or was it just her imagination.

What happened on Carlock...

People had died and she couldn't shake the fact that, somehow, it was her fault. Even though, she couldn't possibly imagine how it could be.

The captain had faith in her. So did Keane for that matter.

But the captain was gone. Disappeared? Taken? Maybe even dead?

And Keane wasn't much better.

So what did their faith in her add up to?

Not much, she figured. Not much at all.

Medication was the only way she was able to sleep now. And neither Rabkin nor Dheer seemed troubled by this. And why should they be? After all, she was suffering from post-traumatic stress disorder.

At least, that was what the therapist on the *Atlantic* had diagnosed her with.

Of course, she hadn't told him about the voice that spoke to her in the darkness whenever she tried to sleep.

No, if she had told him that...if she had told Rabkin or the captain that, they would have kicked her off the ship without a moment's hesitation.

And she couldn't have that.

Calloway couldn't leave the *Defiance*.

She didn't know why.

But every time she considered the idea, the notion, she

immediately tossed it aside. She simply couldn't leave the ship. This was her home now.

Or maybe it was *something else*.

When that ship out there had exploded...that's when *it* happened.

Something, someone, called to her.

At first, she had been certain everyone on the ship had heard it. How could they not have? It had been an overwhelming scream that reverberated across the gulf between the two ships.

Except no one seemed to even be aware of it.

Just her.

Of course it was just her.

After she got past her surprise, she recognized it. It was the distant voice of her dreams. Or her nightmares. She wasn't quite certain which.

So of course no one else could hear it.

For a brief moment, she thought she had fallen asleep at her console. But that couldn't have happened. Not with...everything else that was happening.

But there was the voice. Speaking to her. Or with her? She couldn't tell.

How was she hearing it at all? Why was she hearing it?

It was saying something to her, something important. But she couldn't make it out. Calloway desperately wanted to know what it was saying. She was certain that if she could just once understand, hear, the voice, then maybe it would go away?

Or maybe...

Calloway realized she was crying. Her face was soaked with tears. She made a strangled noise of surprise.

She had to get off the bridge.

Somebody would know. Somebody would *have* to know.

She was clearly going mad and somebody was bound to notice. And when that happened…

The lift jolted to a stop and the door opened with a heavy scratching noise that made her think it was about to fall off at any given moment.

Nobody was on the other side, waiting to get on.

Calloway glanced at the small screen next to the door. Deck eight. Had she selected this deck? She didn't remember. Why would she come to this deck anyway? She didn't know anybody here, did she?

The door stayed open, as though gently encouraging her to step out.

Calloway stepped forward and gingerly tapped the door close command, afraid that she was going to suddenly be zapped with an electrical current.

But the door didn't close.

That was…curious.

Of course, on a good day, the ship wasn't exactly in its prime and today was as far from a good day as you could possibly get.

She tapped the door close command again, with more confidence this time. Although, she still wasn't certain she was going. She had already passed deck six where her quarters were.

The door still didn't close.

Calloway exhaled slowly and stepped off the lift.

She was definitely going mad and she supposed that deck eight was as good a place as any to lose her mind.

9

"*QUARANTINE*?" Dheer repeated, unable to believe her ears.

Rabkin started to seal off the surgical suite. "If he's been infected by the Unity-"

"He was *attacked*."

"There's not much of a damn difference," Rabkin said.

The locks on the surgical suite clicked into place and it went into quarantine mode.

Dheer looked at Keane's unconscious body on the other side of the observation window. "You can't be serious."

"I've never been more serious in my entire life," Rabkin said. "If he's been infected by the Unity, we're all dead."

"If he's in quarantine how the hell are we supposed to help him?" Dheer asked.

Rabkin leveled his gaze at her. "We're not. As far as I'm concerned, Keane's a dead man."

Dheer's eyes widened. "No…"

"You've read the same reports I have," Rabkin said.

"Hell, you've even seen the damn thing first hand. Keane should have never left that ship."

"It's not like we had a choice on the matter."

"Yeah, that's something else that's occurred to me." Rabkin folded. "And I like it about as much as I like having to leave a patient for dead."

"You don't seem to be too worked up about it," Dheer snapped.

Rabkin gave her a hard look. "I have a feeling it's going to be a long day," he said. "And there's going to be a lot of shit to get worked up over before the day's over. I need to pace myself."

Keane's vitals jumped wildly. One second he seemed to be on death's door and then the next everything was racing along like he was in the middle of a marathon. Suddenly his body convulsed violently against his restraints.

Dheer lurched for the door, but Rabkin stopped her.

A moment later, Keane went limp again and his vitals dropped dangerously low.

Dheer exhaled a shuddering breath and shook her head. "We have to do *something*."

"Whatever the Unity left behind in his leg is going to infect the rest of his body," Rabkin said. "Once that happens, it's going to get stronger and once it gets stronger, it's going to come for the rest of us."

"You don't know that."

"Yes I do," Rabkin said. "Because that's what's happened every damn time somebody's injured by the Unity. It's a lethal infection that no one recovers from."

Dheer didn't say anything. She knew he wasn't wrong. She could see it with her own two eyes. Keane's left leg was darkening, slowly turning black as streaks of something slowly worked their way up from the open wound at his knee.

Dheer glanced at Keane's vitals. Her hands may not have been steady, but her mind was still just as sharp. She did the calculations fast. Maybe an hour, maybe less before it reached his spine.

A desperate thought occurred to her.

Dheer sucked in a sharp breath of air. "We can amputate."

Rabkin looked at her as if she had just suggested they all join hands and sing the sickness away. "I beg your damn pardon?"

"We need to amputate his leg," she repeated, more urgently this time. Dheer nodded, as if growing more certain of her idea with every passing second.

"Now I know you're out of your damn mind."

She pointed at the screens. "Look how it's moving through his system. Yes, it's moving quickly, but it's also contained. If we amputate now, we can save him."

"The man's already lost a damn arm," Rabkin pointed out.

"I think he'll prefer it to losing his *life*."

"Whoever goes in there is going to risk contamination," Rabkin said.

"Then I guess whoever does it is going to have to do it *fast*," Dheer said. There was a challenge in her eyes.

"And what do we do with the leg?"

"Shove it out the airlock," Dheer said. "What the hell do I care?"

Rabkin looked at Keane's body. "That's a hell of a gamble. We don't know what kind of long term damage the Unity's already done to him."

"I know he's lost at least one limb," Dheer said. "And if he's lucky, he'll only lose another."

Rabkin pointed to Keane's vitals. "I don't think you're

thinking as clearly as you think you are. You say it's contained, but you don't know that. Our diagnostics can't get a proper reading on the infection. We don't know what kind of internal cellular damage its already done on him. We could cut off his leg and still not get all of the infection."

"Do you have a better idea?" Dheer asked him. "Other than just leaving him to die?"

Rabkin stared her down. "I'm trying to point out to you that we could cut off his leg and he could still end up *dead* and you seem to be disturbingly fine with the fact we could play butcher for no good reason."

"I know damn well that I'm grasping at straws here," Dheer said. "But I'm not ready to just let him *die*."

"Here's a valuable life lesson for you: I know your endgame is to be a CMO one day. It's an admirable goal. Nothing wrong with being the one in charge."

"I don't think this is a particularly good time to go over my career goals," Dheer said through gritted teeth.

Rabkin wagged a finger at her. "Don't interrupt me." He glanced back at Keane for a second and then continued. "One day, you're going to be CMO and you're going to learn that as CMO, you're not just concerned about the patient that's on your table. Sometimes you're going to have to weigh the wellbeing of the rest of crew against one patient."

"Then let me go in there and do it." Dheer held up her trembling hands. "It doesn't have to be perfect to save him. Seal us both in. If anything goes wrong-"

"Then we'll have lost two damn good people," Rabkin cut her off. "I don't particularly like those odds. Especially when you consider the fact we've already lost Mitchell and God knows who else."

Dheer looked at him, her eyes pleading. "We have to do *something*."

Rabkin sighed and turned back to the observation window, watching Keane's body convulse. "Yeah, you're not wrong about that."

10

WARRICK STARED out at the emptiness of space, through a hole that shouldn't have been there.

The forcefield that protected deck ten and, subsequently the rest of the ship, shimmered slightly with a blue haze, as if gently reminding Warrick there was still something between him and the empty void.

It wasn't a big hole and Warrick wasn't a large man. He could have easily stepped through it without having to duck his head. Not that he was eager to do so. It didn't matter, of course. In space, a hull breach the size of a dime was just as dangerous as one big enough for a Vulderran elephant.

Warrick had spent most of his life in space. He felt more at home cruising among the stars than he did on any planet, including the one he had been born on.

That said, he wasn't much of a fan of space.

It was an empty, never-ending void that, with good reason, terrified him. Warrick spent much of his life actively not thinking about how the only thing that separated him from the cold, sterile embrace of space, was a couple feet of thick ablative armor plating.

And then, every so often, a ship he was on would end up with a hole in it and, suddenly, Warrick was reminded how thin the walls really were.

A cold shudder ran down his spine.

The silence of space seemed to leak through the force-field and for a few moments, all Warrick could hear was the sound of his own breathing.

Then everything snapped back into focus.

Sparks dropped from the ceiling and Warrick winced, taking a step back from the hull.

He glanced around the corridor, examining the section of bulkhead surrounding the breach and the huge sections of the ceiling that were dangling so low he could practically reach up and yank them down without even bothering to stretch.

Warrick folded his arms. "Well, ain't that a Fim'ai shit weasel."

"Sir?" A blonde haired lieutenant by the name of Temple stood behind Warrick.

The edges of the hole were charred black and melted into dull lumps. The forcefield was being projected from inside the ship. The only way the repair team was going to be able to patch it back together was from the outside.

"The ablative plating along this section of the ship is shit," Warrick said gesturing to the walls of the corridor. "And that's the technical term. I've officially recorded it in multiple reports to the captain as such."

Temple paused for a moment. "I'm not sure I follow."

Warrick took a step back from the hole. "We should have lost this whole deck, not just...whatever was here." He paused and stared at the section of the bulkhead surrounding the hull breach. He could just make out the former outline of a recessed door. He looked back at Temple. "What was here?"

Temple glanced at his datapad. "A storage closet."

"Anything important?" Warrick asked.

Temple checked his datapad again. "Nothing on the ship's manifest."

"Shit," Warrick muttered. "Probably going to be months before we find out what was in here and when we do, you know it's going to be somebody's irreplaceable collection of Beorution etched glass."

Temple didn't say anything to that.

Warrick sighed. "We lose anybody?"

Temple shook his head. "It was depressurized for only seven seconds before emergency fields kicked in. Most of this section is storage. Nearest quarters are on the other side of the lift."

"Well, we got lucky." Warrick exhaled slowly. "Damn lucky."

The floor beneath them shuddered and the lights along the corridor dimmed for a split second. Across the hull breach the forcefield flickered as though it was going to abruptly cut out.

The hair on Warrick's arms stood up and his stomach did a flip like it was tumbling through a zero-gravity simulator.

The entire incident lasted less than two seconds and neither of the two men ended up sucked out into the void of space.

Still, Warrick took a step back anyway.

He turned to Temple, who now had a vague greenish tint coloring his cheeks. "What was that?"

Temple took a moment to catch his breath. "We've been experiencing power fluctuations all along the starboard side of the ship." He paused, breathing in through his nose to cover the sudden urge to vomit. Once it passed, he continued, weakly, "I've got Schonhorn working on rerouting power to make sure all the emergency systems stay running."

"Great," Warrick muttered. "We're gonna have to EVA this shit. Put together a three-man repair team."

Temple frowned, checking his datapad. "I don't know that we have three men available. Hell, I don't even know if we have two guys available."

Warrick looked at him. "It's a *hole* in the side of the damn ship, Temple. I don't care what other problems we have; we make sure we've got three men to go out there and fix it."

Temple nodded, avoiding Warrick's gaze. "Right. Yes, sir."

Warrick started down the corridor, putting as much space between him and the hole as quickly as he could, without it being terribly obvious to Temple. He paused after a few feet and turned back around. "Temple?"

"Yes?"

"Make sure Westin isn't part of the repair team. Last time she took an EVA walk she nearly walked off into a damn asteroid."

As he rounded the corner towards the lift there was another power flicker. The lights momentarily dimmed, and Warrick held his breath, reaching for something to grab on the bulkhead wall on the off chance that the force-field was going to fail this time.

But he didn't go anywhere.

Warrick exhaled slowly.

The power flickered two more times before he reached the lift.

He wasn't feeling optimistic about what he was going to find in engineering.

11

WHEN CALLOWAY CAME TO, she didn't know where she was.

In addition, she hadn't realized that she had been unconscious.

Except…

Calloway looked down at her feet and hands. She was standing. She had been standing. Maybe walking even? She couldn't have lost consciousness and stayed standing. So clearly, she hadn't lost consciousness. Except…

Calloway searched her memory and realized that the last thing she could recall was getting off the lift on deck eight.

She looked around her location.

This definitely wasn't the lift.

This was…

Where the hell was this?

She brushed a hand through her bright red hair, checking for any lumps. Maybe she knocked her head on something?

It was a large, open space that reminded her of a cargo bay. Except it didn't look like the cargo bay she was familiar with. Did the *Defiance* have a secret cargo bay? Was that a thing? Secret cargo bays?

Calloway shook her head. No, that wasn't a thing. Not on a ship this size.

But still…

Carefully, she moved around the stacks of grey crates that were all larger than her. She wasn't certain which direction she was headed in, but her gut said that it was towards a door and a door would probably explain a lot to her.

Her gut?

Like she should be listening to that. How the hell did she even get down here in the first place?

Naturally, her gut didn't have an answer.

Of course.

There was a shudder under her feet and around her the crates groaned as though they were threatening to topple over.

Calloway picked up her pace, trying to navigate her way out of wherever she was with less of a sense of panic and more of one of confidence.

She turned back to her gap in her memory, trying to find something. She was on the lift, freaking out…

Freaking out? Freaking out about what?

Calloway came to an abrupt halt as she realized she couldn't remember why she had even been on the lift in the first place.

She had been on the bridge. The vessel they had been sent to investigate had exploded and then…things had happened and for some reason she had left her station? But why had she left her station? And why had she come down here, wherever here was?

Calloway raked her fingers through her hair. Something wasn't right.

Something in her *head* wasn't right.

Her recent memories, everything from the alien ship exploding to now was either hazy or just a blank. That wasn't...

That wasn't...

She held a hand to her chest, suddenly realizing she was having difficulty breathing. A panic attack?

Then there was the distinct sound of a large door opening and then closing. It snapped her back to the here and now. The concerns over her memory quickly fading into the background unnoticed.

Calloway turned around in circles, trying to figure out where the sound of the door had come from, but it was impossible to see anything over the stacks.

Finally, she gave up any pretense of pride and cupped her hands around her mouth, and shouted, "Hello? Is anybody in here?"

There was no response.

Calloway was beginning to think she had imagined the door, when she suddenly found herself face to face with the devil peeking around a stack of containers.

Calloway screamed.

Immediately, her face turned bright red with embarrassment, and she took a step back, her hands covering her mouth.

"Sorry," she whispered.

Zemble frowned. "It's not the first time. It won't be the last. What are you doing down here?"

Calloway looked around again. "Well, that depends."

"On what?"

"Where 'here' is."

Zemble didn't say anything for a moment. "Cargo Bay Two."

"Cargo Bay…Two?" Calloway repeated. "We have two cargo bays?"

Zemble held up three fingers. "We have three. Although the third one was sealed off and turned into a secondary workspace for engineering." He paused and asked with genuine concern, "Are you okay, Erin?"

"I…" Calloway exhaled, puffing out her cheeks. "I have no idea how to answer that."

"Do you know what you're doing down here?"

Calloway just shook her head. In her mind, all she could picture was a blank spot where there should have been memories of what happened after she stepped off the lift.

"Come on," Zemble said, guiding her towards the exit. "Let's go down to sickbay."

Something clicked in her head at the mention of sickbay and Calloway stopped abruptly. "Wait a minute. What are *you* doing here? You're supposed to be in sickbay yourself."

"I don't have the time."

"What's that supposed to mean?"

"It means after whatever happened on that ship, Keane's in the ICU," Zemble said. "Since I'm the next ranking officer in security, I'm in charge."

Calloway shook her head. "No, you just suffered some kind of…thing."

"Rabkin kicked me out," he replied.

"He can't do that, can he? I mean, you got…sent somewhere and a…traumatizing thing happened to you," Calloway said. "Right? I think I got it right. Maybe?"

"I'll have time to process it when we're not in the middle of an emergency."

"Which is when? Because, in my admittedly short period of time on this ship, we seem to be very short on downtime." She shook her head. "You shouldn't be up and about. You can't be up."

"And yet, I am."

"And you're in charge."

"Of security. Not the ship."

"Still it's…"

"Rabkin needed the bed for people who were actually injured, which is what I'm thinking you are."

Calloway shook her head again. "What? No. No, I'm fine."

"You're fine?"

"I think."

Zemble grunted. "I don't think I have to tell you that that doesn't sound very convincing."

Calloway nodded, rather surprised with herself at how easy it was to not share a rambling anecdote of how she had apparently lost a whole chunk of her memory.

"Right." Zemble frowned, folding his arms. There was a low rumble at the back of his throat. "Okay. You asked me where you are. You didn't know this was Cargo Bay Two. So how did you end up down here?"

Calloway bought herself a few seconds slowly inhaling and then exhaling, puffing her cheeks out again. She wagged a finger at him. "That's actually a good question."

"It's why I'm Keane's second."

Calloway pressed her hands together. "What would you say if I said I'd rather not answer that question?"

Zemble shook his head. "Come on. I'm taking you to sickbay."

Calloway didn't move, holding up both of her hands. "Seriously, I really don't need to go to sickbay. I swear. I wouldn't lie about something like that."

"I heard from Cammilleri in the science labs who

heard it from Nurse Wieneke that you have an irrational fear of doctors," Zemble said.

Calloway swallowed. "First off, it's not irrational. If you heard the whole story, you'd realize that it was very rational and normal. Second, your questions are making this out to be a bigger deal than it really is."

"I'm starting to feel like it's a bigger deal than I thought it was."

"What are you even doing down here?" Calloway asked.

"Inventory," Zemble said.

"This seems like a weird time to be doing inventory," Calloway replied. "Also, it seems a little out of your, you know, wheelhouse."

"A bunch of main systems are still down, including comms. We've got people on every deck taking a visual on all the crewmen."

"Oh," Calloway whispered, suddenly understanding. "So, a different kind of inventory."

Zemble's voice softened slightly. "How did you end up down here, Erin?"

Calloway paused. Her shoulders slumped forward. "I...don't remember." She leaned against a stack of crates and rubbed her face. "I honestly don't remember. One minute I'm getting off the lift and the next I'm here, in a cargo bay I didn't even know we had. That's probably not a good thing, is it?"

"No," Zemble agreed. "But at least it's not as bad as ending up in some dimension where you can't breathe."

"Right. Perspective."

Zemble wrapped an arm around her shoulder. "Come on. Let's get you to sickbay."

12

IN A FIT OF ANGER, Dheer smacked the console in front of her, hard enough to rattle the mug of Elwat spice coffee sitting to her right.

On the screen, the diagnostics recommended a forty-seven percent chance of success and then flickered.

Dheer held up both hands and took a deep breath.

Forty-seven percent wasn't bad.

It wasn't great. But it wasn't bad. She had performed successful operations with less.

"This is doable," she said to her empty office, purposefully ignoring the warnings listed under potential infection threats.

She looked up at the main screen adjacent to her desk where Keane's real-time vitals were listed. They had continued to fluctuate wildly until settling down into something she was less than thrilled with. Everything said that he was still alive, but not by much.

Time was not on their side.

Whatever they were going to do, they were going to need to do it fast.

Dheer turned back to her desk screen.

And this was going to be their best chance at success.

Then the screen went completely blank and the overhead lights soon followed.

"No," Dheer whispered. "What the hell?"

Her office was pitch black.

In the main medbay a patient screamed as the pain management systems shut off. Panicked voices drowned out the scream as everyone tried to figure out what had happened.

Dheer barely heard any of it. All she could think of was Keane.

She was still breathing, which meant life support was still active. She wasn't floating to the ceiling, which meant the gravity plating hadn't failed.

But they were definitely suffering some kind of power outage.

Dheer tried to remember which power systems the quarantine protocols ran off and came up blank.

She jumped to her feet, waving her hands around wildly, not entirely certain what she was looking for. Her fingers smacked at something and a moment later she heard the telltale sound of her mug striking the floor and breaking.

Dheer swore out loud and, as if in response, the lights came back on.

She glanced down at the screen. It took an extra second, but eventually it powered back up and, unfortunately, none of her data had been saved. All the diagnostics she had loaded on Keane had disappeared completely.

"Dammit," she swore.

Keane's vitals reappeared on the main screen and nothing seemed to have changed.

Dheer rushed out of her office, ignoring the calls from

the nurses and orderlies and raced back to Keane's quarantine room.

Nothing had been disturbed. Keane still lay on the bed, unconscious and strapped in place.

Dheer breathed a small sigh of relief and tapped at the comm. "Engineering."

All she got was static.

Frowning, Dheer tapped the comm again and said, "Warrick?"

Again, she was only greeted with static.

Dheer made her way back to the main area of sickbay. "Why the hell can't I get a hold of Engineering?" She asked no one in particular.

One nurse, a pale woman with narrow green eyes and jetblack hair was the only one to look up. "Comms are still down, Doctor." When she spoke, her voice had a vague echo to it that managed to grate on Dheer the same way nails on a chalkboard did for Rabkin.

Dheer pinched the bridge of her nose. "Then how the hell are we talking to anybody around here?"

The nurse paused before answering, "We're not. Benson's running messages to the bridge, but that's it."

Dheer sucked in a sharp breath of air, trying to not let her anger get the best of her. None of this was the nurse's fault. "Okay. Where's Rabkin?"

Again, the nurse didn't answer right away. "Rabkin?"

"Yeah," Dheer said through gritted teeth, "The grumpy old bastard who's supposed to be in charge around here."

The nurse looked around helplessly, but nobody jumped to her defense and Rabkin didn't magically appear. "I don't know, Doctor."

"Where the hell did he go?"

The nurse shrugged helplessly. "I don't know."

"Wonderful," Dheer muttered. She pressed her hands together and closed her eyes.

Dheer was not a woman who believed in the power of prayer. In fact, she didn't believe in much of anything she couldn't see with her own two eyes. Reality was as reality was and anything beyond that was for the people who didn't have to worry about who was going to live or die on their operating table.

But now, though…

She wasn't even entirely certain who she should pray to. Her parents hadn't been particularly religious and the total sum of her exposure to the concept of a higher power was the six months she spent dating a pastor from the Evangelical Church of Christ. He was a nice enough fellow, but in the end, she cared more about her career than she did her personal relationships.

But here she was, standing in the middle of sickbay, trying to figure out if there was some entity she should be reaching out to for guidance and advice.

An image of Keane slowly being consumed by the Unity flashed through her mind.

Guidance and advice? What she was really hoping for was a miracle.

A sense of peace settled over Dheer and she knew what she had to do.

Dheer opened her eyes, oblivious to the fact that everyone had been staring at her. She pointed at the pale nurse and an orderly. "You two, prep the surgical suite."

The nurse's eyes widened slightly. "But Doctor Rabkin-"

"Rabkin's not here," Dheer cut her off firmly. "And we don't have any way to get a hold of him. I don't have time to run around the ship looking for him. If we suffer another power failure like we just did, we might lose Keane."

And everyone else. Dheer left that part off.

The nurse nodded, properly chastised. "Yes, Doctor." She and the orderly began to prep the surgical suite.

The sense of peace that Dheer felt almost immediately abandoned her. But she ignored it. Sometimes a decision had to be made. Right or wrong. Good or bad. Something had to be done.

The main doors slid open and Zemble came through with Calloway.

Immediately Dheer noticed there was something off about Calloway. There was a distant, vague look in her eyes.

Before Dheer could say anything, a new alarm started to blare.

Calloway doubled over, clutching at her abdomen. The only thing that kept her from hitting the floor was Zemble's quick reflexes.

An inhuman shriek cut through the alarm, almost drowning it out.

It was a sound that chilled Dheer's blood as she recalled the last time she heard it. She started to race back to the quarantine section

"Doctor!" Zemble exclaimed.

Dheer glanced back at them briefly, her brain desperate to play catch up. Zemble held Calloway in his arms, her eyes rolled back. White foam dribbled from her mouth. But Dheer didn't stop.

Dheer shoved past the pale nurse. Her breath caught in her throat.

Keane convulsed violently against his restraints. Every inch of his skin was pulled tight as the veins threatened to burst. His face turned dark red. The inhuman scream that escaped his mouth seemed to affect every screen in the immediate area. They flickered, threatening to cut out entirely.

And then there was a second inhuman scream.

Dheer turned in horror as she realized it came from Calloway.

13

"THE ION DRIVE IS DOWN."

"Well, shit," Sadler muttered, ducking as sparks from a plasma welder rained down from the catwalk above them.

"Hang on," Warrick said, guiding her away from the repair work to a section of engineering that was less active.

Sadler pointed to the faintly glowing coils in his arms. "Are those important?"

Warrick glanced down at them, as though he just remembered he was even holding the coils and chucked them down a nearby trash chute. "Not anymore." He brushed his hands off. "We've still got sublight speed. But, I'll save you the trouble of doing the math. It'll take us the better part of a month to make it back to the *Atlantic*."

Sadler groaned. "What else?"

Warrick raised his eyebrows. "Well, for starters our comm array looks like a deep-fried Nunzotov wildebeest. The only way we could hail another ship right now is if they pulled up right alongside us so they could see us waving our arms at them," he said. "Also, the hull breach on deck ten didn't come to the party alone. We've got a handful of micro-fractures all along the starboard side. If anybody's been complaining of power losses on that side of the ship, they should be grateful that's all they have to deal with."

Sadler rubbed her forehead. "What's the good news?"

"Oh, I'm sorry. That was the good news," Warrick said. "Did I not make that clear beforehand?"

She glared at him. "Are you serious?"

Warrick gave her a dark smile. "Hang in there, Commander, it's gonna get a *lot* worse." He gestured for her to follow him over to an empty console. He pulled up a schematic of the *Defiance*. "So, the repair estimates. They're not short. Honestly, I don't know if I can get the ion drive back online outside of a dry dock. Maybe I could cannibalize some parts from the long-distance shuttle. But even if that works out, and that is a big, massive, 'if', considering the ion coils in the shuttle just aren't built to handle something as big as the *Defiance*. Hell, they'd probably blow out like a Fe'ihrek firework the minute Nax powered up the engines. But, on the off chance they didn't, between the hull breach on deck ten and the micro-fissures, it'd be a straight up miracle if the ship doesn't just break apart under the stress the moment Nax takes us to lightspeed."

"Wonderful," Sadler muttered.

Warrick ran a hand over his bald head. "Best case scenario? I can get the comm array back online and maybe we can get some help. But there's no way I'm getting that done in anything less than four hours. I was able to get the main power grid back online, but thanks to those micro-fractures, I've got no way of getting any stable power to the array once it's resembling something that can actually send a damn signal. So even if we do manage to get a hold of anybody, we'll be cutting out every other syllable."

Sadler nodded, looking over the report on the screen. "Okay." She took a breath. "So, not entirely impossible."

"I'm sorry, have you not been listening to a word I've said?"

"I've heard rumors of you doing more with less," she pointed out, sounding more desperate than hopeful.

"Rumors?" Warrick grumbled.

"We're still breathing air," Sadler said. "That counts for something."

"Well, you really need to ask me if there's anything worse than the bad news."

Sadler closed her eyes. "I really don't want to."

"Oh, I don't know about that."

"The ship is literally falling apart around us, Warrick," Sadler said. "I don't need any terrible news. The bad news is enough."

Warrick didn't say anything. He just stood there patiently; his hands clasped behind his back.

Sadler opened her eyes and sighed. "Fine. What's the terrible news?"

Warrick pulled up another schematic. This one had dozens of red marks scattered across the starboard side of the ship. "So, you remember those micro-fractures that'll tear the ship apart the minute we jump to lightspeed?"

"Yes, I vaguely recall them," Sadler replied flatly.

Warrick tapped the screen and the number of red marks doubled. "They're getting worse."

"We're getting new fractures?" Sadler asked.

Warrick nodded. "The ablative armor plating on the starboard side is shot. There's nothing physically protecting the hull and while they built this old bird to last, I can't get a work order cleared to refit half the ship. Once we got a hull breach on deck ten, it set off a chain reaction. It's like half the ship is about to crumple apart like Vulderran aluminum."

"Oh, shit," Sadler muttered.

"We've got emergency forcefields in place," Warrick continued. "But with all the power interruptions it's only a matter of time before we start leaking air. And when that happens…"

"What can we seal off?" Sadler asked.

"Deck ten for starters," Warrick replied. Parts of deck nine and eight. But that's gonna be like pissing on a plasma fire. It may take me four hours to get the comm array back online, but if we can't get these micro breaches under control, we'll start losing life support long before that."

14

SADLER FELT SICK. Nauseous, really.

She stopped walking, only a few feet from the lift and leaned against the wall. She took a handful of slow, deep breaths in an attempt to keep herself from spreading her last meal all across the floor.

Sadler was not prepared for this. For any of this. This was…

She shook her head, trying not to think about anything for a moment. Thinking about it made her feel even sicker. So she closed her eyes and focused on nothing except for breathing.

In and out.

In and out.

Vaguely she was aware of the lift arriving and the doors opening, but she didn't bother to open her eyes. The nausea was passing and that was worth looking like she was taking a power nap in the middle of the corridor.

"What the hell are you doing?"

Sadler opened her eyes at the grumpy voice and found Rabkin standing in front of her. His arms were folded, and he looked at her like a professor disappointed in a prized pupil.

Sadler pushed off from the wall. "Just taking a moment to get centered."

"You picked a hell of a place and a hell of a time."

She moved past him and hit the call button for the lift. "Well, it was either that or vomit all over the floor. I figure the crew has enough to worry about without having to clean up my mess."

Rabkin's bushy eyebrows furrowed together. "I've been all over the ship looking for you."

The lift arrived and Sadler stepped on. Rabkin followed.

"I'm taking department reports in person," Sadler said. Raising her voice slightly, she said, "Bridge."

The lift started moving.

"That doesn't seem like a great use of your time," Rabkin said.

"It seemed more productive than asking people to stop what they were doing and come see me to file their report."

"It's an *order*."

She glanced at him sideways. "Excuse me?"

"When you're the one in charge, you're not *asking* people. You're *ordering* them."

Sadler looked at him for a second, not saying anything. She turned to face the doors as the lift rose. "What do you want?"

"For starters, I wanted to know why you weren't on the damn bridge. With the comm down, it's not exactly easy to get a hold of anybody right now," Rabkin said. "I do not have the time to be running all over this damn ship looking for you. Never mind the fact that I'm considerably older than you and having to hunt you down because you won't stay in one place isn't a great use of my golden years. I've patients that need my attention, attention that I can't give them if I'm running all over the gorram ship playing hide and seek with you."

"I wasn't hiding."

"Oh? What the hell do you want to call it?"

"I told you already," Sadler said. "It didn't make sense to have everybody make their way to the bridge for report updates. I was trying to be considerate."

"Considerate? *Considerate?*" Rabkin asked.

She looked at him sideways. "Is there something wrong with your hearing or mine?"

Rabkin folded his arms, glowering at her. "I don't know if you noticed or not, but with Mitchell missing, *you're* the captain now. And while I've never had the dubious pleasure of being a captain myself, I'm fairly certain that being 'considerate' isn't in the job description."

Sadler twitched her jaw back and forth, fighting the urge to snap back. "You found me. What is it you want?"

Rabkin grumbled something under his breath that she couldn't make out.

"We lost six crewmen," Rabkin said.

"Last I heard it was five," Sadler said.

"Ensign Prosser didn't make it out of surgery," Rabkin replied. "I've got another three in critical condition, but they'll be fine. Assuming, of course, we don't get attacked by anyone else out here."

"I don't think anybody even knows where we are," Sadler said.

"Then things are already looking up," Rabkin replied dryly.

"Warrick just got finished telling me that if he can't figure out a solution soon, we're going to start leaking life support in the next four hours."

"I was being sarcastic," Rabkin said.

"I know," Sadler said. "Is Keane one of the ones in critical condition?"

"No. Keane is…shit." Rabkin gave a heavy sigh. "Personally, I think he's a lost cause and hazard to the crew. Dheer thinks we might be able to save him by amputating the infected limbs. She's optimistic. It's what I like about her, but I don't know that she's right in this instance. He's infected with the Unity and that's not going to end well for him or any of us if he stays on board."

Sadler stared at him. "What exactly are you suggesting? That we toss him out the nearest airlock?"

"That's exactly what I'm suggesting," Rabkin replied evenly.

"You can't be serious."

"I'm dead serious. We keep him onboard, there's a fifty/fifty chance we make it. We get rid of him? There's a hundred percent chance the Unity doesn't kill us all."

"You're a doctor, dammit."

"Thank you for reminding me," Rabkin replied. "It must have slipped my mind. You know, what with my advanced age and all."

"You swore an *oath*."

Rabkin glared at her. "Little lady, I don't need you giving me a remedial lesson on the moral dilemmas that come with being a doctor."

"It's *commander*," Sadler said.

"Excuse me?"

"It's commander," she repeated. "Not 'little lady.' I'm the ranking officer on this ship right now."

Rabkin frowned. "Sweetheart, you think I give a damn? Because from where I'm sitting, you sure as hell don't."

Sadler hit the emergency stop and the lift jolted to a

halt. She turned on Rabkin. "What the hell is that supposed to mean?"

"I ain't exactly beating around the bush here. It means we need a *captain* right now and all we've got is *you*."

Sadler's face turned red. She sputtered, unable to find the words to properly convey her anger.

Rabkin pointed at her. "You should know, I told Mitchell you should be his number two."

Sadler jerked back like she had just suffered whiplash. "What the hell?"

"You've got potential," Rabkin continued. "I think you could be a damn fine captain."

"You've got a funny way of showing it."

"You're stumbling around here like it's your first day at the academy," Rabkin said.

"You can't be-"

Rabkin cut her off, uninterested in her excuse. "The crew needs somebody who knows what they're doing."

"Well I'm sorry that's not me," Sadler snapped back.

"Then you need to *pretend*."

"Excuse me?"

Rabkin held out his hands, palms up. "Fake it till you make it."

Sadler just stared at him. "I have no idea what that's even supposed to mean."

Rabkin shook his head. "You think Mitchell magically has all the answers?"

"He sure goes out of his way to make it seem like it."

Rabkin grunted. "He doesn't know what the hell he's doing either. What he does know is not to walk around like a damn chicken with its head cut off. You freak out, your crew freaks out."

"This is *exactly* why I don't want command."

"Should have thought about that before you accepted

the promotion," Rabkin said. "As I understand it, you could have made a fine operations officer. Somebody twist your arm to get into command?"

Sadler folded her arms, not answering him.

"That's what I thought," Rabkin said. "So congrats. You're the captain now. Your crew needs you. Hell, your captain *needs* you."

Sadler rubbed her forehead tiredly and tapped at the emergency stop again. Immediately the lift resumed its course. "I don't know how the hell I'm supposed to get the ship back together, much less find the captain."

"Here's a tip," Rabkin said. "It's not your job to get the ship back together. It's your job to make sure you've got the right people on the job to get the ship back together."

Sadler raised an eyebrow, a half smile on her lips. "Is this your idea of a pep talk?"

"Motivated by purely selfish reasons," Rabkin said. "I have no intention of dying out in the middle of nowhere. I plan to pass peacefully in my sleep preferably with a naked woman half my age by my side."

Sadler turned back to the doors, looking queasy again. "I didn't need to know that last part."

There was a double chirp from Sadler's pocket. She pulled out her communicator with a surprised expression. "Warrick must have gotten the internal comms back up."

Rabkin's own communicator started chirping. "This would have made my life a lot easier forty minutes ago."

Sadler opened her comm. "Go for Sadler."

Zemble replied, "Commander, we have a situation down in sickbay."

Both of Rabkin's bushy eyebrows went up as he answered his comm. "What?"

"Old man," Dheer said, her voice sounding strained. "You better get your ass back down here fast."

15

"OKAY," Sadler said, rubbing her eyes. "Somebody want to explain this to me one more time? Only this time, maybe we can do it in a way that makes sense?"

When nobody answered her, she looked up to find Rabkin, Dheer, Zemble and Nax just sitting around the conference table quietly.

"This is not reassuring," Sadler said.

"There's no version of this where anybody walks away feeling assured about anything beyond their own certain and inevitable death," Rabkin replied.

"Is there a version of this where you don't lay on the gloom and doom so thick?" Sadler asked.

"Nope," Rabkin replied simply.

Dheer leaned forward, looking like the conference table was the only thing keeping her upright at this point. "Part of the problem is that we're not all operating with the same set of information."

Sadler looked at her, surprised. "Excuse me?"

Rabkin gave a tired sigh. "Dheer…"

Dheer waved him off. "For starters, Calloway's infected with the Unity."

Sadler jolted in her seat. "When the hell did this happen?"

"Back on Carlock," Dheer started.

"Actually," Rabkin interrupted, holding up a finger, "it's been suggested that it may have started a little bit earlier."

Now it was Dheer's turn to be surprised. She gaped at Rabkin. "I beg your damn pardon?"

Rabkin leaned back in his seat, one hand resting on the surface of the table. "Our friend Steve strongly suggested that Ensign Calloway was infected by the Unity before she ever left Earth."

"Bullshit," Dheer said.

Rabkin shrugged. "No arguments from me on that front."

"How the hell is that even possible?" Sadler asked.

"There's been no Unity outbreak on Earth," Dheer said. "And if there was-"

Rabkin held up a hand, cutting her off. "I know, I know. We should all be dead. I'm just telling you what I heard. Considering the source, let's not buy into it just yet."

Sadler shook her head. "Somebody's going to need to back the hell up and tell me what the hell is going on?" She looked at Zemble. "What do you know about this?"

Zemble fidgeted in his seat. "Very little. All Keane explained to me was that Calloway was being brought into the Security Division for observation. He didn't explain why."

Sadler turned to Nax. "You?"

Nax paused before answering, his eyes flicking around the room briefly as though he was looking for something. Slowly, he shook his head. "This is news to me as well."

Sadler turned back to Rabkin and Dheer. "Great. So it's basically the two of you." She held out her hands, palms up. "Who wants to go first?"

Dheer started to open her mouth, but Rabkin cut her off. "Commander, are you familiar with the concept of classified information?"

Sadler glared at him. "Seriously? This is how you want to do this? After the crap you gave me in the lift?"

"It's a need-to-know basis," Rabkin said.

Sadler smacked her hands against the table. "I'm pretty sure I need to know!"

A faint smile tugged at the corners of the old man's lips.

"You can be a real asshole, you know that?" Sadler said.

"I try my best," Rabkin said. "But it doesn't seem to convince anybody to leave me alone." He looked around the table. "Congratulations. You're all about to be inducted into upper echelons of a top-secret organization. I'm sure this is going to be a nightmare of paperwork for Mitchell, and I ain't gonna lie, I'm going take a small amount of perverse pleasure in that."

The overhead lights flickered but didn't go out.

"Get to the point before we get another hull breach around here," Sadler said impatiently.

"This ship is a Directive Fifty-Two asset," Rabkin said. "And as of this moment, you're all agents of Directive Fifty-Two." He paused and then nodded at Nax. "Well, technically you were already one."

"This…explains a lot," Zemble said.

Sadler swore under her breath. Her hands clenching in and out of fists on the surface of the table. "Are you serious?"

Rabkin just looked at Nax.

"The doctor is correct," Nax replied.

"We're on a damn *spy* ship," Dheer said. "I can't believe this."

"Technically we're on the *only* spy ship," Rabkin said. "President D'Ambra has been on a witch hunt and most of Directive Fifty-Two has been scuttled or been placed under deep cover. As I understand it, we're the only active resource in the field right now."

"And how the hell does this tie-in with Calloway?" Sadler asked.

"Calloway's reaction to the Unity on Carlock set off some red flags," Rabkin said.

"What kind of red flags?"

"She communicated with it," Dheer said.

Sadler blinked and shook her head. "Excuse me?"

Dheer gestured to the viewscreen. "There's some video on file that would explain it pretty concisely, but I'm afraid that if we attempt to pull it up we could end up crashing the half of the ship's systems that haven't gone down yet."

"How is this even possible?" Sadler asked. "Carlock was supposed to be the first interaction we've had with the Unity since the Irac Conflict. How's Calloway already infected?"

"Damn good question," Rabkin said. "According to our scans, she's not. And it's not just our scans, if there was anything off with her she wouldn't have gotten past the initial medical screening for the Academy in the first place."

Sadler turned to Dheer. She nodded slowly in agreement. "She's been under careful observation since Carlock. Not only do our scans show no biological connection within her to the Unity, but she doesn't have any recollection of her interaction with the Unity on Carlock. And it's been the standing order of the captain, against my personal recommendation, that we not tell her."

"A little less editorializing goes a long way, Marlize," Rabkin said.

Sadler looked at Zemble. "Alright. I think this is where you come in."

Zemble adjusted his considerable bulk in a futile effort to find a more comfortable position in the chair. "During my search of the ship I found Ensign Calloway in Cargo Bay Two. She seemed mildly confused and couldn't provide any reasonable explanation as to why she was down there. Beyond that, she didn't exhibit any other signs of sickness or discomfort. But based on her mental condition I decided to bring her to sickbay."

"Where her presence caused some kind of reaction in Keane," Dheer picked up.

"What kind of reaction?" Sadler asked.

Dheer held out her hands. "I don't know."

Sadler raised her eyebrows. "Not exactly what I had in mind when I asked for this to be broken down in a way that makes sense."

"I don't have the words for what happened," Dheer said. "Because there's no precedent for what happened. Calloway's immediate presence in sickbay caused a reaction in the Unity that's infected Keane, which in turn caused a reaction in our systems."

"Half my medical database was just erased like that." Rabkin snapped his fingers.

"Where's Calloway now?"

"Confined to quarters," Zemble replied.

Sadler looked at Rabkin and Dheer. "Is that enough?"

"As soon as Zemble took her from sickbay both Calloway and Keane calmed down and returned to their previous states," Dheer said.

"That's not what I meant," Sadler said.

Dheer shrugged. "I don't know. If Calloway is truly infected by the Unity, and this would be the first piece of proof that we have supporting that hypothesis, she's already had free reign of this ship for months."

Sadler sat back in her seat. "I can't believe this."

"Keane's the pressing concern," Dheer said. "He's literally dying right now."

"And there's no guarantee that cutting off more of his limbs is going to save him," Rabkin said.

"It's a place to *start*," Dheer said.

"I don't know that I would say that cutting up your patient is a place to start," Rabkin grunted. "I don't mean to bring anybody down, but in addition to the damn ship falling apart around us and the fact that two of our crew-mates could turn on us at any moment, we're still missing our captain."

"He's not on the ship," Zemble said.

Rabkin looked sideways at him. "Was that an option?"

"I had Zemble put together a team and, in addition to taking an inventory on the crew, they've been searching the ship for Captain Mitchell," Sadler said.

"Not a bad idea, I suppose," Rabkin said. "But I can't imagine that somebody like Steve would take Mitchell off the bridge with a snap of his fingers only to relocate him to the mess hall."

"I figured we needed to start somewhere," Sadler said.

Rabkin lowered his voice. "Here's a command tip for you, never get into the habit of unnecessarily explaining yourself to your subordinates."

Sadler rolled her eyes. "Nax?"

"Long range sensors are still spotty, but there's no indication of any other vessel in the immediate vicinity," Nax said.

"All of the shuttles are accounted for," Zemble added.

Rabkin looked around the table. "Are we serious right now? We're gonna go down the list of all the possible ways Mitchell could have been taken off the ship? Steve literally snapped Zemble here into a whole 'nother damn dimension."

Everybody tried not to look at Zemble and failed.

"It wasn't as bad as you heard," Zemble said.

"Really?" Sadler asked.

Zemble shrugged. "Technically it was worse."

"Son of a bitch," Rabkin rumbled.

Zemble shifted uncomfortably as everybody stared at him. "I'm *fine*."

"I wouldn't go that far," Rabkin said.

"I'm sure the captain is fine, too," Zemble said less confidently.

Nobody said anything for a moment.

"Warrick tells me that the comm array should be up sooner than anticipated," Nax said eventually.

"Finally, some good news," Sadler said.

"When we get communications back, the *Atlantic* is going to want us to come back immediately," Rabkin said.

"That'll make Warrick happy," Nax said.

"We head back to the *Atlantic*, we'll lose out on any chance we have to find Mitchell," Rabkin said.

"I'm short on options here. The only leads we had either blew up or disappeared into thin air," Sadler said. "I'm not sure how we're supposed to search alternate dimensions we're not even aware of for Captain Mitchell. So, if you have a suggestion, don't hide it under a bushel, old man."

"What's the alternative? We just leave him?" Rabkin asked.

"Leave him? Leave him *where*? I don't even know where

to begin looking for the captain," Sadler said. "We still don't know how Steve got *on* the ship, much less how he got off it. Zemble can't tell us anything about what happened to him other than it was a damn nightmare." She threw her hands up in the air. "I literally have no idea what to do."

"I believe I can help you with that."

Everybody turned to the green haired woman at the far end of the conference table who hadn't been there a moment ago.

"Hello," she said, with a grim expression. "I think I may be able to help you find your captain."

16

SOMEPLACE ELSE...

"Hey, sleepyhead."

Mitchell just grunted and rolled over away from her, trying to go back to sleep.

She pulled herself up next to him, wrapping her arm around his bare chest. She stroked his chest hairs. "Time to get up," she whispered into his ear.

"I have an alarm," he said, not opening his eyes. His voice was half muffled by the pillow. "I don't have to get up until the alarm goes off."

"Well, okay, sure. I suppose that's a valid excuse." She kissed the back of his neck. "But, counterpoint: isn't this a better way to wake up?" She slid her hand down from his chest to his waistline under the covers.

Mitchell rolled onto his back, catching her wrist before it went any further south.

"Hey," she said, giving him a playful smile. "You can't possibly be that desperate for an extra fifteen minutes of sleep that you'd forgo some intimate time with your wife. I mean, it's not that boring already is it?"

Mitchell didn't say anything. His breath caught for a

moment as he tried to focus on a handful of details all at once.

Her hand in his grip. Her soft skin.

The familiar feel of her body against his.

The sensation of *normalcy*.

Except…

He looked at her, his eyes scanning her face with a sense of suspicion and a lack of passion.

She pulled her hand back. "What's the matter?"

Mitchell didn't answer. He threw the covers off and got to his feet. He looked around their room. It was familiar in a way that it shouldn't be.

Something in the air didn't smell right either.

"Are you feeling okay?" she asked. "Do you want me to call Jim?"

There was a window across from their bed. The view was of a class two nebula. That nebula…

He knew that nebula. And the last time he had seen it was over a decade ago.

"What the hell is this?" he asked, not turning around to face her.

"Excuse me?" she said.

Everything was laid out the way it was supposed to be. Or, at least, the way he remembered it. Except, he knew that his memory wasn't exact.

There were books on the shelves, but they didn't have any titles on the spines.

Thirteen years ago the nebula had been a kaleidoscope of interstellar dust and hydrogen gases, colliding together in rainbow-colored micro explosions. What he saw out this window was flat and almost dull, like an uninspired rendering produced by a simple computer algorithm.

"Gavin?" she asked. "If this is supposed to be some kind of joke, I'm not laughing."

Mitchell took a breath, steeling himself and finally turned back to the woman in his bed. "Who are you?"

Her expression turned from confusion to anger. She sat up and the sheets slid down to reveal her naked body. Mitchell's gaze didn't move from her eyes.

"Last time I checked, I'm your *wife*," she replied. "Although, you're starting to have me question whether or not it's worth keeping the job."

Mitchell didn't reply. He didn't know what to say. Everything felt right and wrong all at once.

She got out of the bed and grabbed a robe. "I don't have time for whatever this is. I thought we could have a little bit of together time this morning considering that we're not going to see each other for a month. Clearly I was wrong."

Automatically, without even thinking about it, Mitchell reached for her. "JoJo-"

She stepped out of his reach, tightening the belt of her robe. "No. I don't know what the hell kind of game you're playing, Gavin, and right now I don't care. I have to get ready. My shuttle leaves at oh-nine-hundred and I still have some packing to do."

She disappeared into the other room, leaving Mitchell alone in their quarters.

He stared out at the nebula.

This wasn't right.

But it wasn't wrong, either.

Mitchell closed his eyes, cupping his hands around his mouth.

A pain stabbed at his abdomen and he doubled over, dropping to his knees.

Around him he felt the room spin.

He opened his mouth to call for her, but instead-

17

MITCHELL JOLTED UPRIGHT, spilling out of the bed as he vomited. He caught himself with his hands on the cold concrete, the greenish liquid from his mouth splattering across the floor. He tried to pick himself up and his arms gave out almost immediately.

"Hang in there," a voice said.

Another sharp pain stabbed him in the abdomen and Mitchell curled up into a ball as his stomach muscles seized. More green liquid came up.

Rough hands grabbed him by the arms and carefully helped him up.

"I'd tell you it's okay, but we both know that'd be a bald-faced lie," the voice said, helping him back up onto the bed. "Take a deep breath. Slowly, though. You don't want to push yourself. The air's thinner here than you're probably used to."

The bed, which was hardly any more comfortable than the concrete floor, sat against a wall. Mitchell let the wall handle the hard work of keeping him upright at this point.

Mitchell tried to speak, but his voice was hoarse and

scratchy. His throat hurt the moment he even tried to make a sound.

"Don't worry about it," the voice said, patting him on the shoulder reassuringly. "Give it a few minutes."

His vision blurry, Mitchell closed his eyes, rubbing them and then looked around again. Everything was mostly in focus now.

There was a man in front of him. He looked to be in his fifties, possibly older. His head was mostly bald and there was a white, scruffy-looking beard covering his face. His skin was almost as white as his beard and he dressed in an outfit that looked like it had been cobbled together from the contents of a trash bin.

The man looked at Mitchell with the keen eye of a doctor examining a patient. He pressed his thumb at the skin under Mitchell's eye and pulled down on it slightly, checking the edges of his pupil. The man nodded, frowning. He pointed a finger at him. "Don't move."

He stepped away to a small counter across the room.

Move? Mitchell wanted to laugh. He couldn't even think about moving. He looked down at his hands. They tingled faintly, as though he had briefly lost circulation. Sensation was slowly returning. The rest of his body felt the same, vaguely numb and weak. No, he wasn't going to be moving, at least not for a few minutes.

"Here," the old man came back with a cup of something and handed it to Mitchell. "Drink it. Fair warning, it's not going to taste great. So your best bet is to down it all at once."

Mitchell took the cup hesitantly; not entirely certain his hands were up to the task of not dropping it. But his grip tightened around its base and after a second it felt perfectly normal in his hands.

He lifted the cup towards his mouth and then jerked back at the rancid smell of its contents.

The old man nodded. "Yeah, it doesn't smell great either. But it's the best you're gonna get considering the circumstances."

Mitchell wanted to ask what he meant, but his throat still hurt too much to speak.

The old man tapped the bottom of the cup, gently lifting it towards Mitchell's mouth. "Go on. Trust me. It'll help with your throat first."

Mitchell gave him a dubious look.

The old man held up both hands. "Hey, I'm just trying to help you, stranger. You can do it the hard way, but it's going to be worse than the few uncomfortable minutes this is going to be.

Mitchell frowned. His legs were starting to feel a little more normal. But the rest of his body still had the vague tingling to it.

He lifted the cup, wincing again at the rancid smell, and quickly gulped it down.

Mitchell coughed violently. The juice burned going down his throat and he could almost feel it thickening before it ever reached his stomach, as though it was attaching itself to his insides, soaking through his membranes.

His eyes watered and he lurched forward.

The old man patted him on the back. "Yep. That looks about right. Give it another minute and you'll start to feel like more like your old self."

After a moment the burning sensation passed. The feeling of the liquid weighing down inside him passed shortly after that. His body was starting to feel more normal, although every inch of him ached as though he spent the last twenty-four hours being beaten nonstop.

Mitchell slowly sat back against the wall, watching the old man as he watched him. Something tugged at the back of his mind and he was having a hard time getting to it.

His throat was still burning slightly, so Mitchell took the time to look around the room as he let the rancid juice do its job. It was small. Structured like an exam room. The walls had a rough, brownish hue to them, as though they had been carved out of coarse unforgiving stone. They looked smooth, but Mitchell could feel the imperfections on his back. Tiny empty pockets of space mixed in with smoothed over bumps, as though somebody had gotten tired of running a sander over the surface halfway through the job.

There was the bed, which was only a little softer than the floor. A small counter that held a collection of aged bottles and what appeared to be some gauze tape. To the right there was a closed door with an ancient looking handle.

There didn't seem to be any diagnostic equipment. In fact, near as Mitchell could tell, there didn't seem any technology in the room at all.

Wherever he was, he wasn't on his ship.

Mitchell exhaled slowly. He coughed again, this time it was less violent and more like he was trying to clear his throat.

"Your color's returning," the old man said. "That's a good sign."

Mitchell carefully swallowed and winced slightly. "Who…are you?" His voice was barely above a whisper. It still hurt to speak, but not nearly as much as it had before the rancid drink.

The old man stuck out his hand. "Schiavinotto. Although, around here everybody just calls me Otto."

"Otto," Mitchell repeated, shaking his hand slowly. "Nice to meet you. Captain Gavin Mitchell."

"Captain?" Otto replied with a wide-eyed expression. "Well, there's a fancy word you don't hear too often around here."

"And where exactly is here?" Mitchell's voice was starting to sound more like its normal self.

Otto didn't answer right away. He tilted his head to the side and watched Mitchell, as though he was waiting for something else.

"What?" Mitchell asked. "I say something wrong?"

Otto folded his arms. "Well, that really depends on how you want to look at it."

Mitchell cocked an eyebrow. "What's that supposed to mean?"

"Well, stranger, from my point of view, you just showed up out of nowhere," Otto said. "And given the circumstances around here, I really think I should be the one asking you where you're supposed to be from."

"Circumstances?" Mitchell asked.

Otto's gaze narrowed. "You really don't know?"

Mitchell rubbed his eyes tiredly. That thing at the back of his mind was nagging him again, but he still couldn't quite get at it.

"Okay," Otto said after a moment. "What's the last thing you remember, Mitchell?"

"I…" Mitchell trailed off, searching his memory. Things were strangely fuzzy. There was a woman's face, but he couldn't quite place a name to it. He tried to make out the details, but they were shrouds in a foggy haze. He shook his head. "A woman? I think?"

"Well, there are worse places to start." Otto smiled. "She a pretty woman? Maybe she's got a name?"

Mitchell rubbed at his temples. "I can't remember."

Otto nodded. "See, that helps things make a little more sense."

Mitchell looked at him sharply. "I do remember I don't like playing games."

Otto held up his hands in the universal sign of 'Calm down.' "Hey now, I'm just the guy that saved your life. I ain't the one stuck you in that airlock."

Airlock?

Mitchell sat up a little straighter. "What airlock?"

"The one you were found in, obviously," Otto said.

An airlock?

That thing tugged at the back of his mind again and Mitchell tried to tug back, but it slipped through his grasp.

Mitchell looked at him suspiciously. None of this made any sense. He started searching the pockets of his uniform.

"Looking for anything in particular?" Otto asked.

"My communicator," Mitchell said. "I need to contact my ship."

"Your...ship?"

Mitchell's search came up empty. "You got something you want to say?"

"Just that I would very much like to see this ship of yours," Otto said. "Considering, well, it's been quite some time since we've seen a starship around here."

"What's that supposed to mean?" Mitchell asked.

"I'm not mincing words here, Captain Mitchell," Otto replied. "You're telling me you've got a ship? Well, I'm telling you that you might have hit your head a little harder than we thought. It's been nearly fifty years since the last starship passed through our little galaxy."

18

"*Captain?*" The word came out of the Oxean's mouth with all the grace of a swear. "Captain Gavin Mitchell?" The Oxean looked at him suspiciously and it took every ounce of Mitchell's will power not to lunge across the room at the man. His thick, pale lips smacked together. He spoke slowly and carefully as he tried to speak over his own thick accent. "Captain of *what* exactly?"

The room they were in was domed shaped, carved out of the same material as the rest of the place. It was like walking through a series of underground caverns to get anywhere. But there was no echo. Whatever kind of stone this place had been carved from, it absorbed every sound, storing it away in some unseen cavern.

Mitchell stood in front of what Otto called the Council. It was made up of six people. Three women and three men. Most of them were human, save for the Oxean and an alien that Mitchell had never seen before. They were all at least as old as Otto appeared to be. The youngest, one of the women, appeared to be in her mid to late sixties.

Mitchell had never seen an Oxean as old as this one

before. Historically speaking, the Oxean people didn't care much for their elderly and had a terrible habit of killing them off once they became too much of a burden.

This Oxean, though, didn't look like he was about to be anyone's burden, despite his age. His pale, chalky skin was peppered with dark, shadowy patches that had a fuzzy look to them. He was bald save for a few strands of black hair that had been braided together in what appeared to be an attempt to convey some sense of authority. There were a series of rings piercing the holes that ran from his forehead down to his cheekbones. His eyes were a hazy gray, but sharp, nonetheless.

The Oxean and the rest of the Council were all dressed like Otto. Haphazard outfits pulled together from a variety of sources. He spotted logos, uniform pants and shirts that looked almost threadbare.

The Council.

The Council of what?

The way Otto had spoken of them, it suggested they were in charge. But this didn't look like a group of people in charge of anything other than a homeless shelter.

Mitchell leaned on a cane Otto had provided. His legs still felt wobbly and the walk from the exam room to this new location had taken longer than he would have liked. He felt himself slowly getting better and he figured he could get rid of the cane within a couple of hours. But better from what? What happened? How did he go from the *Defiance* to here? Wherever here was?

The Oxean's lips smacked together impatiently. "I asked you a question, *Captain*."

Mitchell tightened his grip on the cane. It was better than balling his hands into fists.

"I'm Captain Gavin Mitchell of the United Planetary Alliance vessel the USS *Defiance*," he said.

The Oxean barked out a laugh. "What the hell is this supposed to be, Otto? Your idea of a joke?" His words started to slur together under his thick accent.

Otto just shrugged. "I'm as flummoxed as you are."

The Oxean pointed an accusatory finger at Mitchell. "How did you get here?"

"I'd like to get an answer to that myself," Mitchell replied.

The Oxean smacked the table in frustration. "We should have just killed him and been done with it."

"Can't say that one comes as a surprise," Mitchell said under his breath.

One of the women spoke up. "You'll have to forgive Vix'amar." She was the youngest one in the group and sat immediately next to the Oxean. Her hair was strawberry blonde, but white streaks were starting to overwhelm it. The wrinkles around her eyes and mouth were almost soft, as though they were being smoothed out over time. She spoke with an even tone that could have been mistaken for compassionate, if not for the current circumstances.

"Do not presume to speak for me, Savina," Vix'amar snapped, his slur getting worse. "I meant exactly what I said. We should have just let him die and moved on with our lives."

"Not to be that guy," Mitchell said. "But there's a big difference between killing somebody and just letting them die."

"Not these days," Otto said out of the corner of his mouth.

Savina shot both Vix'amar and Otto a disapproving look that spoke volumes. Otto looked appropriately shamed, but Vix'amar appeared to double down on his attitude. He folded his arms and just grunted.

Savina turned her attention back to Mitchell. "This is

a…well, *unique* situation we find ourselves in." She gave him a half smile. "And honestly, we're not quite sure how to react."

Vix'amar grunted and sat back.

"I'm not sure what I'm supposed to tell you," Mitchell said. "I'm looking for the same answers myself."

Savina turned to Otto expectantly.

"He doesn't seem to be suffering from any kind of brain damage that I can ascertain," Otto said. "There seems to be some mild amnesia, but it seems mostly focused around the issue of how he got here. He also doesn't seem to be aware of the overall situation here. And, most importantly, as our initial scans indicated, he's completely free of any infection."

Vix'amar grunted again. "That's proof of nothing."

"Well, for starters, it's proof that he's not going to kill us all," Otto said.

"And if we had killed him at the beginning of all this, we would have the same results," Vix'amar pointed out.

"Again, big difference between killing me and letting me die," Mitchell said. "And I'm not particularly fond of either one of them."

Vix'amar sneered at him. "Well, I'm not particularly fond of you, *human*."

"Vix'amar," Savina warned him.

The Oxean smacked the table again. "No! What is the point of any of this? Who cares? Toss him back out the airlock and let the Hawia have him."

"That's remarkably shortsighted, even for you," she said.

Vix'amar made a noise at the back of his throat, glaring at her. He got to his feet and spat at the floor in front of Mitchell before stomping off.

She turned back to Mitchell. "He's not big on change."

"Okay," Mitchell said. "How 'bout instead of talking about me like I'm some kind of mystery to be solved, somebody gives me some damn answers."

Savina folded her hands on the table, briefly looking at the rest of the Council. When none of them seemed to register any objection, she turned back to Mitchell. "Captain, you present a bit of a mystery for us. As I'm sure, Otto here has already mentioned, starships are a thing of the past now."

"He made a reference to that," Mitchell said, eyeing the Council warily. "Not that it makes any sense."

Savina nodded. "It does when you consider that everything is of the past these days. Do you have any idea where you are?"

Mitchell shook his head. "And nobody seems eager to tell me."

"This is Apaka Twenty-Two-Twenty-One," Savina said.

It felt like everyone in the room was collectively holding their breath.

Mitchell looked around, confused. "Is that supposed to mean something to me?"

Savina glanced at Otto, who shrugged. "I don't know what to tell you," he said.

Savina paused before saying anything else, as though she was searching for the right words, the right combination of words to express some terrible notion. When she looked at Mitchell again, her eyes were soft.

"You remember nothing?" she asked. There was almost a pleading tone in her voice, as though she was looking for some excuse, any excuse, to not have to do something.

"I remember everything leading up to whatever happened that brought me here," Mitchell said, flexing his grip around the cane. "I remember my entire career with the UPA. I remember my childhood. I remember the *Defiance* and every one of my crew. Whatever it is you people think I'm supposed to know, I don't know. And I sure as hell wish somebody would just tell me already."

Savina exhaled slowly, nodding her head. "Captain Mitchell, *Gavin*, we're concerned, confused and, admittedly, a little hopeful at your presence because we're all that's left," she said. "Quite frankly, we can't conceive of the notion that you have no idea where you are, considering there's no place else in this universe for you be. Gavin, you are the first person who's stepped foot onto our little home in nearly fifty years. Apaka Twenty-Two-Twenty-One and her small population are all that's left in our universe."

19

MITCHELL HEARD THE WORDS, but he couldn't make any sense of them. He understood them, he understood what they were *supposed* to mean. But, logically, he couldn't grasp what they *actually* meant.

Savina got up and moved around from the table, gesturing to an empty chair. "Perhaps you should sit down."

Mitchell shook his head, holding up a hand to keep her back. "What the hell are you talking about?"

Her lips pressed together into a thin line of determination. She turned to the other Council members and nodded at them. Two of them got up, the alien Mitchell wasn't familiar with, and a bulky man that looked to be in his mid-seventies. They both walked to opposite sides of the room and gripped cranks that Mitchell hadn't noticed before.

As they wordlessly turned the cranks, the domed ceiling slowly opened, separating at a seam down the middle.

It took a few minutes and even after the dome had

been mostly pulled back, Mitchell wasn't entirely certain what he was looking at.

He wasn't sure where they were. It was a ship, that much was certain. They weren't moving through space. But neither were they planet-bound. Despite the cave-like structure of the place, it didn't *feel* like a planet.

Which left, what?

Mitchell wasn't certain.

But at the very least, he figured once the dome was open he could get some idea as to where they were based on the view of the stars.

But there was nothing there to see.

No stars.

No hint of atmosphere.

Nothing.

Just…darkness.

He stared at the darkness for what seemed like a small eternity. It pulled him in, like an inviting abyss. He could see nothing in the darkness, but at the same time he realized he was seeing *everything*.

After what felt like forever, but in reality had only been a few seconds, Mitchell realized the darkness was *moving*. Undulating against…something?

What was out there?

Mitchell shivered, but didn't feel cold.

Slowly he blinked and, almost regretfully, tore his gaze away from the darkness. He looked around the room at them. The thing at the back of his mind bothering him even more now. But every time he reached for it, it would slip out of his grasp.

They all stared up, transfixed by the darkness and Mitchell realized they were all feeling the same thing he was. The same…*pull?*

Mitchell noticed one of the men silently crying and seemingly oblivious to his own tears.

The other woman on the table had her hands pressed together as she looked up at the darkness almost reverently, her lips moving silently. Mitchell was unable to make out what she might have been saying.

Otto gazed into the darkness with an expression of tired wonder.

Mitchell felt the urge to look back up and he fought it, knowing instinctively that nothing good would come from it.

Eventually, Savina made a noise at the back of her throat. It wasn't a cough or an effort to clear her throat. It was like a startled grunt, as though she suddenly remembered she was still awake, still alive.

"Basavappa, Dalleore," she said quietly, but loud enough for the two men at the cranks to hear. They made similar noises as their attention was pulled from the darkness and they began rewinding the cranks, closing off the dome.

The dome slid back into place with nary a sound. Distantly, though, Mitchell imagined he heard a faint *click* as locks were turned.

Nobody spoke for a few minutes. Nobody looked at anyone, not even Mitchell. There was a sense of shame that filled the room.

"It's been that way for almost fifty years," Savina said eventually. Her voice was quiet, like she was afraid of disturbing the peace. But it slowly returned to a normal volume the more she spoke. "For a couple of years after we settled here there were a few stars you could still make out." She pointed up towards the closed dome, presumably in the direction of where the stars had once been. "But they soon faded away, too. I don't think there was anybody out there then, though. At least I hope there was no one out there." She lowered her gaze back to Mitchell. "Which makes you all the more interesting."

"I don't understand," Mitchell said, his voice sounded hoarse again. His fingers kept flexing against the cane, as though they were searching for an answer.

"It's been this way for nearly three hundred years," Savina said. "They worked their way across the universe, consuming everything they came into contact with. Every person, planet, and piece of technology. They even ate the *stars*." She sounded almost breathless. "We are literally the last surviving group of *anything* here. We stopped receiving transmissions almost immediately. Even the ancient radio signals from Earth. They just *stopped*. We think they ate those, too. There was one group of refugees shortly after we settled here. They were desperate for asylum. There were only, what? Twenty of them on the small ship?" She looked to Otto for confirmation. He nodded. "Twenty. A mix of human and Veneer. It was a miracle they had lasted as long as they had, but we couldn't risk letting them onboard. They could have been infected already. That long out there, trying to outrun them? They *had* to be infected. So we didn't let them in."

Savina paused, her voice trembling. Even now, decades later, the memory of turning away the last survivors of their universe troubled her.

She took a breath, wiping at the tears that collected at the corners of her eyes but refused to fall. "And then you appear. As if out of thin air, right in an airlock that hasn't been used in fifty years and wasn't planned to be used ever again. So tell me, Gavin Mitchell, how did you survive the Hawia?"

Hawia?

Something clicked in the back of Mitchell's mind. He

stumbled back under the sudden weight of his memories flooding to the forefront of his mind. Otto caught him and guided him to the chair he had refused a moment ago.

His ship was in danger. The *Defiance* was...

The Eternal Hand of God.

The Unity.

"Steve," Mitchell whispered.

Confused, Savina tilted her head at Mitchell. "Steve?" When he didn't answer, she turned to Otto "Are we supposed to know who Steve is?"

20

USS DEFIANCE

Nobody at the table moved.

The memory of what happened the last time somebody had rushed an entity that had mysteriously appeared out of thin air was still fresh the minds of Sadler, Rabkin and, especially, Zemble. Dheer and Nax, while they didn't have the shared experience of having watched as Zemble was snapped away to another dimension and then back again, were still appropriately cautious regarding the green haired woman.

"I'm sorry," she said. "I wasn't really sure what the best way to announce myself was."

She was, objectively, the most beautiful woman any of them had ever seen. There was a glow to her skin that seemed to illuminate the room. She sat rigidly at the end of the table, her posture perfect. Hands with long, slender fingers rested casually on the table. Her green hair was swept back, cascading down her shoulders in luscious curls and shimmering almost separately from the glow of her skin.

The woman's eyes were the exact shade of green as her

hair. It created a disconcerting effect for the crew *Defiance*, even though none of them were consciously aware of it.

Her lips were full and pressed together in an expression that none of them could quite identify. She seemed to be in the room, without actually being present. They all observed her but couldn't connect with the fact that she was there.

She raised a carefully groomed eyebrow. "Did I say something wrong? Should I perhaps leave and come back? Maybe announce myself over your comm channels? Would that be more appropriate?"

Dheer was the first one to finally speak. "The hell kind of question is that supposed to be?"

The green haired woman shrugged. "One in which I was attempting to be...considerate?" She paused, tilting her head to the side. "Is that the right word? Am I using it correctly?"

Zemble slowly got to his feet, careful not to make any sudden moves.

The green haired woman watched him, studying his body language. "Ah, yes. I see. I've done something wrong."

"That's one of way putting it," Sadler said.

The woman zeroed in on Sadler. "Are you the one in charge now?"

Sadler shifted uncomfortably, trying not to look at Rabkin. "Yes," she said with her best command voice. "In the absence of our captain. I'm Commander Sadler of the *USS Defiance*. Would you care to tell us who you are?"

"I'm," the woman at the table paused for a moment. She raised both eyebrows in mild confusion. "Well, I'm not entirely certain what the best way to answer that question is."

"That's never a good sign," Rabkin said. "Doesn't bode well for the rest of our interaction here."

She took another second, looking at them, a nearly vapid look on her face. She blinked and her expression shifted, regarding Sadler with an intense look. "Recently you were visited by someone...different than yourselves, yes?"

Rabkin and Sadler looked at each other.

"That's putting it mildly," Sadler said.

"Is there a more appropriate way to put it?" the green haired woman asked. "Your method of communication, your language, is confusingly simplistic."

"I'm not entirely certain, but I think she just called us stupid," Rabkin said.

"Is that considered a bad thing?" she asked.

"Traditionally, yes," Rabkin replied dryly.

She bowed her head slightly. "Then you have my, apologies? Yes? I believe that's the correct word? It's not my intention to offend."

Sadler and Rabkin shared another look.

"Okay, well, I'm out of ideas right now," Rabkin muttered under his breath.

Sadler shifted in her seat, pressing one hand against the surface of the table. "Steve," she said. "The person you're talking about who visited us was Steve."

"Steve?" The woman smiled in mild surprise. She folded her hands together. "Well, okay then. Let's say that I'm 'Steve's' sister."

"You have a name?" Sadler said. "Because if I'm going to have to call you Steve's sister I'm going to have some serious flashbacks to some awkward friendships I had back when I was ten."

The green haired woman pressed her lips together thoughtfully. "A name? Well, as I'm sure *Steve* already explained to you, my name isn't exactly something you can easily pronounce."

"He made a production out of the announcement," Rabkin said.

"Yes, that sounds like him," she replied. "His sense of…" She trailed off as her eyes got a momentary distant look before focusing back on the room, "*dramatic flair* doesn't often win him any friends."

"Dramatic flair," Rabkin repeated. "I like that. Granted, it sure as hell undersells the sociopathic part of him, but I can't deny it hits the nail on the head."

Sadler looked at Zemble and nodded at his chair. "Sit down."

Zemble didn't move.

Sadler sighed. "Zemble, if she is who she says she is, it's not like you're going to be able to do anything anyway."

"All due respect, Commander, but that doesn't sound like very sound security advice," Zemble said, not taking his gaze from the green haired woman.

"Maybe it's not, but it's pretty practical," Sadler said. "The only people you're intimidating is us and, hell, I'm feeling more uncomfortable than intimidated. So, please, just sit the hell down."

"If it helps at all, Commander Sadler," the green haired woman said. "I'm not here to harm anyone. My intention is simply to provide aid and assistance. After all, if I wanted to do anything untoward you, I wouldn't have bothered introducing myself in the first place. Also, to be entirely truthful, I can't say that it's really worth my time to cause you harm."

"I can't decide if we should be relieved or insulted," Rabkin said. "You people have a real way with words."

"Thank you," she replied.

"It's not a compliment," Rabkin said.

Zemble slowly returned to his seat, his gaze not once moving from the green haired woman.

"Okay," Sadler said. "Now that I don't have him looming over my shoulder, I'd still like to know what to call you."

"Some time ago I was given the name 'Sharon' by the residents of a lower dimension," she said. "I presume that will suffice here?"

Sadler and Rabkin looked at each other.

"I'm sorry, *Sharon?*" Sadler said.

She nodded. "Is that not a word you are familiar with in this dimension?"

"Oh, we're very familiar with the name," Sadler said. "I had an aunt who went by that name."

"My daughter's name is Sharon," Rabkin said.

"Then this is a good thing," she said.

"Not particularly," Rabkin said. "Sharon's the one I don't like very much."

"And my aunt had a bizarre thing for poisoning the neighborhood pets," Sadler said.

Rabkin looked at her. "What?"

Sadler shook her head. "It's really not a thing I want to get into right now." She focused on the green haired lady. "The point is, it's not exactly the kind of name we would associate with an entity that claims to be from a higher dimension."

"If you'd like, we can determine a new designation for me," she said. "But that doesn't seem as though it would be a very good use of my time, considering I'd rather not stay here any longer than I have to." She looked around the conference room with thinly veiled distaste. "Your dimension is…not ideal."

"Yeah, she's definitely related to Steve," Rabkin said.

"Okay," Sadler said. "Sharon it is."

"Well that's great," Dheer said impatiently, getting to her feet. "While we're all sitting around playing naming games and getting useless history lessons, I've got a patient who's *dying*."

Sharon's face brightened. "Yes, that's an excellent place to start."

Dheer looked at her, confused. "Excuse me?"

And then everyone in the room disappeared.

21

"I HOPE YOU DON'T MIND," Sharon said. "I assumed time was of the essence and it was faster this way."

The six of them had abruptly appeared in the middle of sickbay. A nurse gave a startled scream and dropped a tray of medicine.

"What the hell was *that?*" Rabkin asked, grabbing the closest bed for support. He felt nauseous as the room spun around him.

Sadler pressed her hands to her temples and squeezed her eyes shut, taking a few deep breaths. For her, the room wasn't spinning so much as it felt as though gravity could abandon her at any moment.

Dheer abruptly vomited, grabbing at her abdomen.

Nax blinked but appeared otherwise unaffected.

Zemble was simply upset. He growled at Sharon and moved between her and his crewmates. "Don't try that again."

Sharon glided past him without a second look, heading towards the quarantine area. "Your crewman is sick."

Dheer wiped at the corners of her mouth and straightened up. She glanced at Rabkin. He waved her on. "I'll be fine as soon as the rest of my brain gets the message I'm not holding on to an oversized spinning top."

Dheer followed Sharon. "He's dying."

"Yes, death means something here in this dimension," Sharon said. "That's quaint."

"*Quaint?*" Dheer grabbed the green haired woman by the shoulder, yanking her around so they were face to face. "Quaint? I don't know where the hell you're from, but that's not how we describe death around here. We treat it with a little more damn respect."

Sharon looked distastefully at Dheer's hand on her shoulder. She reached up and plucked it from her as though she was touching a dirty rag. "While I am not here to offend or harm you in any way, I would strongly suggest that you not touch me in that manner again. As for how you handle the issue of life termination, I don't particularly care. I simply used the word 'quaint' in an effort to be polite. Next time I will not bother."

She turned and resumed her walk to Keane's quarantine area.

Dheer glanced at Sadler as she came up beside her. "Who the hell is this bitch?"

Sadler pressed her thumb against her left temple, massaging it. "Her name's Sharon. Did you miss that part?"

Sharon stopped outside the observation window of Keane's quarantine zone. She wore an expression of disappointment. "Oh." She turned to face Dheer and Sadler. "He's been infected by the_____."

Dheer clutched at her ears and winced in pain. She couldn't make out the word Sharon had said. But it had done something to her ears nonetheless. It was a sharp, stabbing piercing that echoed through her eardrum. Her eyes rolled back briefly as a violent twitch ran down her body.

Out of the corner of her eye she saw Sadler have a similar reaction.

And then it stopped.

Sharon frowned at the two of them, watching them with a detached sense of confusion. "Ah, yes. That's right. They're called something different here. The *Unity*?" She nodded. "Well. That's certainly an appropriate name for them." She turned back to Keane. "Though, it lacks a certain brutal, unrelenting ruthlessness that's at their core."

Dheer swallowed, working her jaw back and forth as she tried to pop her ears. "What the hell?" she gasped.

"You would do best to get him off this ship," Sharon said. "Not that it would do much to help your crewman. But it would certainly give the rest of you a chance to escape."

"That's not an option," Dheer said.

Sharon turned to face Dheer, her face empty of any recognizable emotion, but yet Dheer could still detect a sense of disapproval.

"It should be," Sharon replied. "The...*Unity* is not something you should keep in the vicinity of...Well, *anything*. It's an inter-dimensional parasite that knows no limits. The fact that it hasn't consumed this vessel and everyone on already is...interesting." She turned back to the observation window and leaned closer. "Why aren't you all dead?"

Dheer wasn't sure what to say to that. She turned to Sadler, who just shook her head. "I'm about six steps behind here," she admitted.

Dheer took a deep breath, trying to steady rattled nerves that were dangerously close to their breaking point.

"Oh, this is very interesting," Sharon said, leaning close

enough to the window that her breath should be fogging it up, but there was no indication that she was even breathing.

Dheer heard something in the green haired woman's voice, something that she latched onto immediately. "What?" she asked, trying to keep the desperation out of her voice and failing. "What do you see? Something, right? You see *something*?"

"I see many things," Sharon said. "A great many things that you don't. It wouldn't be productive for me to list them all. Also, you wouldn't understand most of them."

"Dammit!" Dheer snapped. "You said you could *help*."

Sharon clasped her hands behind her back. "And perhaps I can." She tilted her head. "This is very curious and unexpected. What's wrong with it?"

Dheer pushed her hand through her dark hair, brushing it back behind her ear, in an attempt to distract herself from how shaky her hand had become. She spoke quickly and almost frantically, as though at any given moment she was going to run out of words. "He was attacked by the Unity on a vessel from another universe. I think in the process of the attack, it infected him, but not on purpose. It could explain why the infection is working through him so slowly. It's an extreme solution, but I think it might be possible to save him by cutting off the infected parts."

"No," Sharon said with a touch of irritation. "Not him. *It.*"

Dheer looked at Keane and then back at Sharon. She shook her head. "I don't understand."

Sharon frowned. "Savages. That's what you are. Blind savages. I could hand you the secrets of the universe and you couldn't even begin to imagine what to do with it." She stepped around to the door and waved a hand over the control panel. All the lights turned green and the door opened.

"What the hell is she doing?" Rabkin barked, racing down towards them.

"You can't-" Dheer started, but it was too late.

Sharon stepped inside the quarantine space, her hands still clasped behind her back and slowly walked around Keane's body.

Dheer cast a nervous glance at Keane's vitals, but nothing appeared to be any different. His heart rate was a little lower than it had been earlier, but everything seemed relatively steady. Everything in her screamed to go in there, to stop the green haired woman, to do *something*. But Dheer didn't move.

Sharon held a hand out over Keane's body. Nothing happened.

Zemble came up behind Rabkin. "Should I remove her?"

"I don't know if we really have a choice in the matter," Sadler said. "What are you going to do that'll be different from when you tried to remove Steve?"

Zemble growled under his breath.

"Not meant as a slight against you," Sadler said. "Just trying to remind you that you're not exactly the most effective solution against these people."

"Still sounds like a pretty effective slight against me," Zemble replied.

"What the hell is she doing?" Rabkin asked.

"This is rather amazing. I don't believe I've ever seen this before." Sharon's voice came through the open door and over the speakers at the same time. "There's something wrong with it." She looked up at Sadler and the doctors through the observation window and smiled. "Your crewman may not be a lost cause after all."

"It? What's she talking about?" Rabkin asked. "Keane?"

"No," Dheer whispered as it clicked into place for her. "*It.*"

Suddenly there was a bright burst of light and Keane's body strained against the restraints, bucking upwards towards Sharon's outstretched hand.

Power across sickbay began to fluctuate wildly.

Multiple alarms sounded.

Concerned cries rose up from the nurses and patients.

And in the quarantine room, the light grew even brighter.

Thin, tendrils of a dark ink-like substance were being pulled from Keane's body. They stretched across the distance between the surface of his skin and Sharon's hand.

Keane's eyes shot open and his mouth stretched in a silent scream.

It seemed to go on forever.

The thin tendrils simply grew longer and longer, never ending.

It was impossible to see Sharon through the bright light and soon even Keane disappeared behind it.

But the black tendrils remained clearly and painfully visible.

There was a distant sound, a scream. Something inhuman and human all at once. Something familiar and alien. Later, when Dheer would try to recall it, it would simply be a blank spot in her memory. She would logically know that the sound was there, but she would be unable to give it substance or echo. It would simply be a mark in her memory that would fade away completely over time.

And then the light was gone.

Sharon stood there, smiling. In her hand she held a

greenish orb, no bigger than a tennis ball. "What a fascinating development."

But no one was paying any attention to Sharon.

The focus was now on Keane.

The restraints had fallen away, and he sat up, staring down at two hands where there had been only one.

22

Nax didn't move from the main area of sickbay. He didn't trust himself to. Instead, as Zemble and Rabkin raced after Dheer and Sharon he stepped back out of the way until he reached an empty spot along the wall.

Nobody noticed him. They were too busy focusing on Sharon.

Nobody except for Hawkins.

She sat on an empty bed, swinging her legs back and forth. "It should go without saying that you probably shouldn't trust her."

Nax didn't look at her.

"Oh, come on," Hawkins said. "How long are you going to ignore me?"

Nax took a deep breath and pressed the tips of his fingers together. His lips moved as he silently recited an old Natuzzi meditation prayer his mother had taught him.

"That's not going to do anything," Hawkins said. "And I think you know that." She hopped off the bed. "Let's be realistic here. Not only do you know that's not going to do anything, but you don't *want* it to do anything."

Nax stopped and finally looked at her. Making direct eye contact with a woman he knew to be dead.

"Except, if I were dead, would I be here?" Hawkins asked. "Talking to you? This isn't how dead people behave is it?" She held up a finger and wagged it as if suddenly remembering something. "That's right. You don't believe in death. Or the afterlife. You believe in *universal harmony*. Whatever the hell *that* is supposed to mean."

Nax decided he couldn't take it anymore. Without a second glance back, he quickly stepped out of sickbay and into the corridor, taking long strides towards the lift.

"You know you can't just walk away from me," Hawkins said, keeping pace with him.

"But it has come to my attention that you can walk away from me," Nax replied.

Hawkins placed her hands on her cheeks in mock surprise. "You're actually speaking to me! *Gasp*!" She looked around. "What will the crew say if they see you talking to thin air? Oh, that's right, they don't know about Fey's Euphoria. So if nothing else, you can just pass it off as a weird Natuzzi thing. You've done that quite a few times."

Nax reached the lift and pressed the call button with more force than intended.

"Careful, Warrick has enough to fix around here."

Nax stayed focused on the closed doors of the lift, refusing to look at her.

"Oh, no," Hawkins said. "Did I say something wrong? Did I offend your delicate sensibilities?"

The lift arrived and the doors shuddered slightly before opening.

"Well, I'm not going to lie," Hawkins said, watching Nax step into the lift, "If I were still alive, I'd be real hesitant about stepping into that thing."

Nax looked pointedly over her head at the empty corridor until the doors slid shut.

"Deck three," Nax said and with another shudder, the lift started moving up.

"I take it back." Hawkins was standing next to him again. "You should definitely feel free to bang this thing up a little more. It shouldn't be in service. It's clearly a death-trap waiting to happen. If Warrick isn't going to shut it down, the responsible thing for you to do is to damage it in such a way that nobody can use it until it's fixed." She looked at him with a deadly serious expression. "You're the next ranking officer on this ship. You're basically the new first officer until the captain makes it back. Making sure your crew isn't under the threat of a lift crashing on them is literally the least you can do."

Finally, Nax turned to her. "Both Doctor Rabkin and Warrick outrank me."

"But neither of them are next up in the chain of command," Hawkins said. "Also, unless you were going to put a fusion pistol to their heads, neither one of them is going to volunteer to take command should something happen to Sadler. And, let's face, at this point something is bound to happen to her. Even if she wasn't less than underwhelming as acting captain, she faces a very real risk of losing her life to a faulty lift around here."

"And if Captain Mitchell doesn't return?"

"The captain's coming back."

He looked pointedly at her. "What do you know that we don't?"

Hawkins shrugged. "Probably nothing. Considering I'm simply a figment of your diseased mind."

Nax bristled slightly. "My mind is not diseased."

Hawkins arched a bemused eyebrow. "Oh? And what do you call it when you're talking to your dead lover?"

Nax didn't have a reply to that.

She shrugged. "It's fine, you know. Personally, I don't think there's anything wrong with you. But then, I'm biased." She turned to face the lift doors. "You know, plenty of Natuzzi have lived long and productive lives after being diagnosed with Fey's Euphoria." She paused and then added, "Well, I suppose that 'productive' is a bit of a stretch. But you're not on Natuzzi anymore, so maybe you shouldn't be so afraid of the stigma? You know, as I understand it, the Sweezakaals hold their mentally ill in very high regard. I mean, they elected one to be their Prime Minister, that's got to count for something, right?"

"You said you know where the captain is."

Hawkins looked at him out of the corner of her eye with an impish grin. "Did I?"

Nax studied her for a moment, trying to figure out what it was he was really seeing.

"You're seeing exactly what you're seeing," Hawkins said. "There's no smoke and mirrors involved here."

"Personally, I think you should be more concerned with Sharon's intentions rather than Captain Mitchell's wellbeing." Hawkins paused. "Although, I suppose I could just call him Mitchell now. Or maybe Gavin? That sounds weird, though, doesn't it?" She made a face. "It's true what they say, old habits do die hard."

"This isn't like you," Nax said.

"Maybe death's changed me," she suggested.

"That would imply you're not simply a figment of my diseased mind," Nax said.

"I don't know about you, but off the top of my head I can't think of any species that considers the ability to commune with the dead as a good thing," she replied. "Or maybe this is how you always saw me."

"That's not true."

She frowned, her eyes chastising him. "This should go without saying, but there's really no point in lying to a figment of your imagination."

"Humans lie to themselves every day." It sounded bizarrely weak coming from him.

"That's true," Hawkins agreed. "But we don't usually have a separate personality that's taken up residence in our mind calling us out for lying to ourselves."

"You don't know where Captain Mitchell is," Nax said.

"Of course I don't," Hawkins replied. "I'm not really here. I'm just a result of neurons misfiring in your temporal lobe."

Nax pressed his lips together firmly. "It doesn't feel particularly euphoric."

She shrugged. "Euphoria is in the eye of the beholder, yes? The Fornien find the experience of chemically castrating their elders to be overwhelmingly euphoric."

"That is an…ill-advised example."

"It's the best your mind could come up with."

Nax closed his eyes, unable to look at her any longer. "I can't do this."

"Well, you're going to have to do something," Hawkins said, her voice sounding oddly distant now that he couldn't see her. "Because Sharon isn't going to just leave you alone if you ask nicely."

"I am less concerned with Sharon then I am with *you*," Nax replied.

"Oh? And what is it you think you have to do for me?" Hawkins asked.

Nax wordlessly pressed the heels of his hands against his eyes.

"So far I haven't asked you to do anything," she said. "Other than not to ignore me and that doesn't seem like anything too unreasonable."

"But it is," Nax said. "When it's you."

"Aw, that's sweet," she replied.

"No, it's a nightmare," Nax said, his voice barely above a whisper.

"Maybe, but I don't think you're really thinking this through."

He opened his eyes and looked at her. "In what regard?"

She smiled and a bittersweet, aching sensation swept through him. He opened his mouth to say something, but he couldn't think of anything to say.

Hawkins stood up on her toes and kissed his cheek.

For the briefest of moments, Nax imagined he could actually feel her lips.

"See?" she whispered, "That's not so bad, is it?"

And then Nax was alone again.

23

APAKA 2221

Mitchell needed time.

His memories rushed over him like a raging river. And as quickly as they returned, they settled down.

Everything clicked back into place.

But he needed *more* time.

His body still ached. Legs still felt a little unsteady, but he felt himself slowly returning to normal. Despite this, he didn't move from his seat. He kept both hands wrapped around the handle of the cane, clutching at it in a way that suggested one or both of his legs were far from steady.

Mitchell took a couple of deep breaths under the guise of appearing confused and physically overwhelmed. And, technically, he was both. Except now…

He cast his gaze around the room at the remaining Council members a little more cautiously, with a little more suspicion.

Steve had sent him here. There was no question about that in his mind. What was it he had said?

"And now, Captain, we do it the hard way."

The hard way? What the hell had that meant? Was *this* the hard way? It sure as hell didn't feel easy.

And what happened before? In the time between Steve taking him from the *Defiance* and waking up here, wherever here was? Had that been real? Was that really JoJo? Mitchell searched his memory, trying to draw up as much detail about it as he could, but it kept slipping away. He could remember that it happened, but the details felt sketchy and vague. It had certainly *felt* real at the time and even now, as it was disappearing behind a hazy cloud it still felt more real than some of his past memories? But was it real? It couldn't have been, could it? There was a memory, an older memory, that was similar. Something from before. But this, this had been different. It didn't feel like a memory. It felt like something *different*.

Mitchell needed more time. Time, judging by the expressions on the council members, he did not have. And what little time he didn't have couldn't be spent lost in thought about his ex-wife. He needed to focus on the here and now, the immediate threat. And there was no mistake about it, this was definitely an immediate threat.

He needed answers. Starting with whether not he had a ship to even go back to. When Steve had taken him, the *Defiance* was too close to the *Eternal Hand of God*. Sadler was warning that shields wouldn't hold against the blast. What had happened to his ship? To his crew? Were they even alive?

"Mitchell?" Otto asked, checking his pulse. "Can you hear me?"

"Yeah, I can hear you just fine. There's nothing wrong with my ears." Mitchell waved him off and slowly got back to his feet. He made a show of using the cane to support himself.

He needed to prioritize. Deal with what was in front of

him. Address the issues that he could. And right now, he didn't even know where the *Defiance* was, much less where he was. He was going to have to trust that if they were able to, his crew would survive. Right now, he needed to focus on his own survival.

Steve brought him here. Why? Were any of these people in league with Steve? Could he trust any of these people? Were any of them even real? Was that something Steve could do? Create whole people out of nothing?

Mitchell mentally chided himself. Whatever Steve was, he wasn't a god, no matter what he insisted. Steve was just another alien. He had some inventive tricks up his sleeve, he may not have to put his pants on one leg at a time, but he was most definitely not a god.

So if Steve wasn't a god and he didn't create these people, then that meant they were real. *This* was real.

Mitchell glanced up at the dome, where the darkness lay beyond, surrounding them. *That* was real.

"Mitchell?" Savina said. "You seem a bit lost."

"I'm feeling lost," Mitchell replied.

Savina nodded almost sympathetically. Did she truly understand or was she just being polite? Or worse, was she pretending? Playing a role written by Steve and waiting for Mitchell to slip up?

"Who's Steve?" she asked. There was something in her voice that sounded genuine. Mitchell instinctively wanted to trust it and so he fought against that urge.

"I have no idea," he answered truthfully.

Savina and Otto shared a look. Mitchell tried to decode it, capture the message underneath it. They had clearly known each other for a long time and had mastered that ability that only the oldest of friends had to communicate without even talking. The details escaped him, but the broad strokes were pretty clear: they were troubled by something. He didn't blame them. If he had been in their position, he'd be troubled, too. Never mind the fact that according to them, he had appeared out of nowhere. If what they had shown him on the other side of the dome was true, if it wasn't some kind of trick or illusion, these people were completely surrounded by the Unity.

24

"Here, drink this."

Mitchell looked suspiciously at the cup Otto handed him, the memory of the last drink Otto had given him still painfully fresh in his mind.

"Don't worry," Otto said. "It's just water. Or, at least what passes for water around here."

"I'll pass," Mitchell said.

Otto shook his head and set the cup down on the table between Savina and Mitchell. "Trust me, you're not going to want to." He twirled a finger to indicate wherever they were. "The rocks around here have a tendency to pull more moisture from your body than you're likely used to." He tapped the rim of the cup. "This is your best, and more importantly, your only option to keep from shriveling up into a very unappealing piece of beef jerky."

"Otto," Savina said with a tired sigh.

Otto held up both hands in surrender and moved to a chair set against the wall.

Savina had moved the three of them to a small room adjacent to the council room. It was carved out of the rock-like substance. The chairs looked a little more comfortable than what he had experienced so far and judging by the handful of personal touches around the room, Mitchell assumed it was Savina's private office.

On the desk, at a forty-five degree angle sat a photo encased in a black jeweled frame. The frame seemed like a relic from a bygone era. It had a handcrafted appearance to it, matched with an effort in meticulous design that seemed absent from everything else in this place.

The picture itself was of Savina, a man, and young girl between them. Judging by how Savina looked now, Mitchell figured the picture was about twenty years old. The girl between them had to be around thirteen in the photo. Savina's family? Her husband? Daughter?

Mitchell looked at the woman across from him. Surrounded by the other council members, she had appeared almost youthful. Here in her office, contrasted against the woman in the photo, Mitchell became aware of crushing exhaustion that weighted her down.

She nodded at the cup. "It's really not that bad."

Mitchell peeked over the rim of the cup. In the poor lighting he couldn't quite tell what the color of the liquid was. "Water?" he asked, looking dubiously at Savina.

"Close enough," she replied. "At this point it's probably better for you than actual water."

"Don't let my doctor hear you say that." Mitchell picked up the cup and took a cautious sip. It didn't burn like the last drink, but it wasn't entirely flavorless either.

"I think, given the circumstances, I would love to say anything to your doctor," she replied.

Mitchell set the cup back down. He couldn't identify the aftertaste, but it reminded him of something minty.

Savina took a breath, folded her hands on the table.

Her eyes briefly dancing across the photo before leveling themselves with Mitchell's.

"Gavin, I like to think I'm a pretty good judge of character," she said.

"Everybody likes to think that of themselves," Mitchell replied evenly. "Nobody wants to admit they're the one who can't tell difference between a sociopath and a plain loser."

A smile tugged at the corners of her mouth, but Savina kept herself composed. "Be that as it may, you are in my home."

"So maybe calling you an idiot isn't the best tactic here?" Mitchell asked.

Now she did let herself smile. "See, I was right. You're not a stupid man."

"Thank you, I think."

The smile faded. "But I don't think you're being a truthful man either."

"Can you blame me?" Mitchell asked. "From my point of view, you're just as much of a mystery."

"Fair enough," Savina agreed. "But we're not in your home right now."

Mitchell watched her for a moment, weighing his options. "Your home?"

"Be it ever so humble."

"What planet is this?" Mitchell asked.

"*Planet?*" Savina sounded like she was about to laugh. She shook her head. "There aren't any planets anymore. They're all gone. Along with all the moons. And the stars. All gone."

Mitchell didn't know how to react to that. He understood the words, but their context made no sense. He struggled with the enormity of what she was suggesting.

"Then where the hell are we?" he asked. The question came out more forcefully than he had intended.

Savina didn't answer right away. She kept staring at his eyes, as though she was perhaps waiting for him to break?

"An asteroid," she said finally. "We think it used to be a chunk of a moon back before…Well, back before everything went to Hell. Or, I suppose if we're being accurate, before Hell came to everything. It's small. Only thirty kilometers in length. A little over half of that is even habitable. There's no atmosphere, of course. No oxygen. No water either. We had to retrofit our ship's life support systems to generate a habitable space. Everything is recycled. Nothing is wasted. It's quaint. It's shaggy. But it's home nonetheless."

"Hell of a home," Mitchell said.

"Hell of a time to be alive," she replied. "So…"

"You know, at first I thought the Oxean was in charge around here. Now I'm starting to think otherwise."

Savina gave him a small smile. "Vix'amar is certainly the loudest one around here. He's most definitely not in charge."

"That's probably a good idea," Mitchell replied. "Where I come from, Oxeans aren't the most trustworthy."

"And where is it you come from?"

Mitchell didn't answer.

Savina sighed. "Look, it's obvious you're not telling us your whole story. And while I can understand and even appreciate your desire for privacy, that's not a luxury we can afford here anymore. We took a risk bringing you in."

"I appreciate that," Mitchell said. "But right now I'm not sure I'm prepared to give you more than a kindly worded 'thank you.'"

"And how can you be certain that kind of response won't get you tossed back out into the abyss?"

"Because I know desperate people when I see them," Mitchell replied. "Maybe you shouldn't have spent twenty minutes going on about how I was the first new person to set foot on your little oasis out here in nearly fifty years."

Otto made a noise that sounded like a strangled laugh.

Savina looked down at her fingernails. She wordlessly picked at the corner of her thumb for a few seconds before saying, "There are only one hundred and seventy-five of us left."

Mitchell struggled to keep his expression neutral.

"When we arrived here fifty years ago, we were nearly twice that," she continued. "Our numbers are dwindling. Not because of the Hawia or any contagion." She looked at him. "We simply aren't reproducing."

Mitchell half turned in his chair to look at Otto, but the old man was pointedly looking away from the both of them.

"I don't think I understand," Mitchell said to her.

"It's not that complicated of a concept," Savina replied. "I'm sure that wherever you're from they have sex?" She made a show of looking him over. "You look like the sort of man that's probably intimately familiar with a lot of different women. This can't be that alien of a concept to you."

"Now I'm real confused," Mitchell said. "Are you trying to pump me for information or flirt with me?"

"A little of both," she admitted. "You wouldn't have thought it, the end of the universe is kind of dull."

Otto got to his feet. "I don't actually have to sit around here for this, do I? He's obviously not going to pose any threat to you and this conversation as a whole is clearly moving in a direction that I don't need a front seat for."

Savina waved him out. "We'll meet up with you in the promenade later."

"I'm looking forward to it," Otto replied with a hint of sarcasm and disappeared out the door.

Mitchell turned back to Savina. "What do you think is going to happen here?"

"At the very least, I'm hoping that we can reach some kind of understanding."

"And beyond that?"

"If what you're trying to ask is whether or not I'm prepared to jump your bones right here and now," Savina said. "The answer is no. Try not to look too relieved. After a while of being around the same group of people, certain skills can atrophy."

"And you wanted to make sure you could still flirt?" Mitchell asked.

She shrugged. "It's been a long time since there's been a man around here that caught my eye. What can I say? I'm only human."

Mitchell wrapped his hands around the cup. He didn't drink from it. He just held it. His hands needed something to do, something for him to focus on. This all felt so…

He kept picturing JoJo in a memory he was almost certain wasn't real.

"But you're not the only human, are you?" Mitchell asked, staring at the liquid in the cup.

"No," Savina replied with a heavy sigh. "But we're definitely on the endangered species list."

"How many?"

"Including the half breeds? Twenty."

Mitchell looked up sharply, surprised.

"There's a mix of races here," Savina explained. "Not a huge mix. There's only three Oxeans. One Aurrod. Hardly a perfect sampling of the universe that used to exist. Some of them are compatible. Most are not."

Mitchell nodded. "You're not reproducing."

She shrugged. "It's as though something on our basic cellular level has just...given up. There was a surge of births in the first twenty years. We were all so desperate to find a way to keep going. We were estimating that our population was going to double, maybe even triple by the time we were fifty years old, creating, of course, a whole 'nother problem. Space is limited around here. But over-population was a problem we'd've all gladly struggled with when we were staring down the barrel of extinction." She pressed her lips together, rolling them inwards. "But then, something changed. I don't know what it was. Neither does Otto or anyone else around here with an inclination towards the medical sciences. It wasn't for lack of trying. We all certainly gave it our best shot." She smiled coyly at him. "But something wasn't working."

"That's a hell of a thing to go wrong," Mitchell said.

"Well, it's the end of the universe," Savina said. "So it's pretty much par for the course." She sat forward, an eager look in her eyes, bordering on desperate. "Do you under-stand now? If you are truly from some other place, you could be the solution we've been looking for. Because you can't be the only one."

"Is that what you're hoping for? A breeding farm?" Mitchell asked.

Savina jerked back as though she had been slapped. "That's rude."

"I'm just trying to piece together the subtext here," Mitchell said.

"And I keep trying to give you the benefit of the doubt," she replied. "And in return, you just keep slapping me in the face. I don't know what you think is going on here. I can't imagine who you think I am. But whatever dark theory you've concocted in your mind, it is so very wrong. There is only one enemy here and it's the Hawia.

I'm simply trying to save as many people as I can from an abyss that can't be stopped. Maybe that means you can help. Maybe it means I can help you. Either way, we shouldn't be fighting each other."

Mitchell traced a finger around the rim of the cup, taking a long moment before responding. Finally he looked up at her and saw an earnestness that couldn't possibly be faked.

Or maybe it could, and he was just a fool for thinking otherwise.

Mitchell straightened up in his seat. "It's a little more complicated than that."

Savina chuckled softly. "It's the end of the universe and you appeared out of nowhere. Frankly, at this point I'd be disappointed if it was as simple as discovering another asteroid floating next door to ours."

"Where I'm from," Mitchell said slowly. "We don't call it the Hawia. It's the Unity and it hasn't done to us what it's done to you."

"Well, now it's my turn to be confused."

"I don't think I'm from this universe," Mitchell said.

That was when the alarm sounded.

25

THE ALARM WAS a klaxon that echoed down the stone corridors, each reverb causing Mitchell's back molars to ache.

Savina moved quickly with a surprising amount of grace. Mitchell followed her, racing down the narrow corridor at a quick hobble. He kept a tight grip on the cane and used it to pace himself a good five or six steps behind Savina. His body felt mostly normal again, but despite everything he had learned so far, he was still too cautious, too suspicious, to not hold back a little. If it gave him an edge to have them think he was still recovering, he would take it.

They passed no one in the corridor, which was good considering how narrow the space was. It felt like an afterthought, as though it occurred to somebody they needed to have a way to get from point A to point B without walking across the surface of the asteroid after they had moved in. Mitchell tried to imagine how the Oxean would move through the corridor and conjured up a rather comical image of the loudmouth council member getting himself stuck in the middle.

Despite the effort to hold himself back, Mitchell found himself breathing harder than he should have been.

The path curved sharply and started tilting downwards at an alarming angle. Mitchell had to periodically grab at the wall to keep from falling. Savina, however, moved with practiced ease, never once pausing to catch herself or even bothering to make sure Mitchell was still following her.

Eventually they reached a thick, steel door. It looked like it had been placed awkwardly in the wall. Somebody had carved out a hole for it and then discovered, too late, that it wasn't going to fit. They managed to jam it in there anyway. It sat crookedly in the wall. One corner flush, the other jutting out almost six inches. The bottom was recessed against the stone and Mitchell wondered how it was possible that the door would even open.

There was nothing written on the door to give any indication of what was on the other side. There was, however, a fading logo that seemed vaguely familiar to him: A golden swooping arc that intersected with what used to be a black delta and was now nothing more than a faint outline.

This door was from their ship, he realized. That logo, was it what used to be the UPA in this universe? He wanted to ask, but he didn't have the chance. Savina rapped her knuckles on the door twice and it slowly opened.

The other side was some kind of command center. It was the first sign of any recognizable technology Mitchell had seen. There were a dozen computer stations spread out across the space. Thick tubes of wires crisscrossed the floor, connecting every console and then dozens of other wires disappeared into wide, jagged holes in the walls.

The computers looked old. The screens were fuzzy. Everything had physical controls or buttons. There wasn't a single piece of equipment in the room that didn't look like wasn't over two hundred years old. The computers made ancient noises that he had only heard in movies. Clicks, beeps and whirring fans. He could almost feel the vibrations of each console against the floor. It felt beyond old. It felt ancient. How were these people surviving on an asteroid with equipment that appeared to be hundreds of years old?

Here the alarm was muted, almost a background noise. But the people in the command center didn't move any less frantically. Mitchell counted only seven of them.

"What is it?" Savina asked, approaching the nearest console.

A pink haired woman with dark brown skin and thin gills lining the sides of her neck rushed up to Savina. Her eyes blinked rapidly, changing color each time. Mitchell didn't recognize her species. She was easily the youngest person he had seen around here by at least twenty years. "One of the southeast generators is failing."

Savina tensed. She glanced back at Mitchell for a brief moment. Something flashed across her face that he couldn't identify. Fear? Suspicion? Something else?

Savina scanned the information on the nearest screen. "What happened?" Her voice sounded strained.

The pink haired woman shook her head. "We don't know. Pelikan and Condodina are out there doing maintenance. One of the power coils looked like it had overloaded, but its backup was working fine. The system isn't showing any errors."

"Obviously that's not the case," Savina said. "When was the last time you heard from them?"

The pink haired woman glanced at the time on the screen. "Over three hours ago."

Savina's eyes blazed with anger. "They're supposed to check in every hour."

"I know-"

"What the hell are you doing up here?" Savina snapped. She didn't bother waiting for a reply. She pushed passed the pink haired woman and moved to another console. Its occupant, an older looking Elwat, quickly moved out of the way. Savina opened a channel. She leaned in close to the microphone and said, "Pelikan? Condodina? Do you read me?"

The only response she got was static.

Savina toggled the channel again. "Condodina? Do you copy?"

Static.

Savina smacked the console in frustration.

"What's going on?" Mitchell asked.

Savina didn't answer him. She turned back to the pink haired woman. "Who's in the south section right now?"

The pink haired woman didn't even need to check her console. Her eyes stopped blinking and turned a shade of dark green. "Stuppard's science class."

Savina dropped into the nearest seat, a numb expression spreading across her face. "That's almost half of the children left."

The pink haired woman blinked rapidly, and her eyes matched her hair. "Maybe there's something we can do. The generator hasn't completely failed. We still have time before there's a breach. I can get Leung or maybe Flournoy down there and they can-"

"No."

"But-"

Savina turned to steel. "No. We follow procedure. Seal it off."

For a long second, nobody moved.

Savina got to her feet, glaring around the room. "If we don't seal it off now, we risk damning the lives of *everyone* here. I will not do that. Seal it off *now*."

Everybody started moving.

At some point, somebody turned the alarm off.

The computers hummed along and the floor beneath Mitchell's feet vibrated a little more intensely.

Long minutes passed without anyone speaking. The seven people moved wordlessly, but efficiently. Whatever was being done, they didn't like it, but they were all too familiar with the procedure.

Eventually the pink haired woman stood up again. She looked in Savina's direction but couldn't meet her eyes. "The new southeast generator is running. Everything's green across the board."

Savina nodded, not trusting herself to say anything. She stepped away from the group towards Mitchell. The steel door was still open. In the excitement, no one had bothered to close it. She gestured for him to follow her back out into the corridor.

Mitchell looked around the command center again. There was a sense of gloom that had settled over the room. It was as though he had suddenly stepped into the middle of a funeral.

He turned and followed Savina out into the corridor.

She stood propped against the wall, her eyes brimming with unshed tears.

"What just happened?" Mitchell asked.

Savina didn't answer right away. She wiped at her eyes with the heel of her hand. "In your universe," she said, her voice trembling with emotion. "How bad is it?"

"I don't understand," he said.

She inhaled sharply through her nose and straightened up, pushing off the wall. Whatever moment of weakness he had caught her in was fading. "In your universe, the Hawia…." She paused. "The Unity is what you call them? How much have they taken? What's left?"

Mitchell was almost afraid to answer her. The moment of weakness may have passed, but even he could see she was barely hanging by a thread.

He looked down at his palm, flexing his fingers. "A hundred years ago the Unity made their first strike. Something happened and they weren't able to…" He looked up at her. "I don't understand the science of it, but there's something in our universe that they can't process."

Her jaw twitched as she fought to hold back fresh tears. "You're telling me…" she trailed off, her voice breaking up.

Mitchell nodded slowly. "It's nothing like this. The Unity are barely a threat in my universe."

26

THE PROMENADE WAS the largest open space Mitchell had seen on Apaka Twenty-Two-Twenty-One so far, but it was hardly impressive. It was two levels carved out of the asteroid, centered around what clearly used to be a chunk of their ship that had been refitted into a public meeting area.

Mitchell and Savina sat on the upper level. Ramshackle lighting was strung up along the walls, casting wide, hazy spotlights over the space and creating almost twice as many shadows. Fifteen or so people milled around, doing their best not to stare at Mitchell and failing.

"A whole 'nother universe," Savina whispered. Her hands were cupped around a small glass of whatever Otto had given Mitchell earlier. It was, apparently, the drink of choice around here. She gripped the cup tightly in order to keep her hands from trembling. "I can't even imagine it."

"It's a fairly new concept to me, too," Mitchell admitted.

"Steve?"

He nodded. "Yeah."

"Why do you suppose he brought you here?"

"I don't know," Mitchell admitted. "He plays his cards pretty close to the vest."

"Perhaps he works in mysterious ways?" Savina suggested.

"He's not a god."

"That's not how you described him."

"Then I clearly didn't do a very good job," Mitchell said.

She tapped her thumbs against the rim of the cup. "Our universe used to be home to an untold number of species. To the best of my recollection, not a single one of them could step between universes."

"Maybe they could and were just too modest to tell anyone," Mitchell said.

Savina shrugged, turning her attention back to the cup. "Maybe."

Mitchell glanced down at the open space below. There were two other humans mixed in a group of Vulderran. They kept glancing up at him, much to the irritation of the Vulderran.

"Do you not have religion in your universe?"

Mitchell looked at her, slightly confused. "Excuse me?"

"Religion," Savina repeated. "Is that something that exists in your universe, or…"

Mitchell took a sip from his cup. It was just as flavorless as the one Otto handed him. Again, there was a hint of mint in the aftertaste. "Oh, we have plenty of religion. Steve's not a god."

"Have you ever met a god?"

"Have you?"

She took a hand from her cup and waved it towards the ceiling, in the direction of the asteroid's surface. "There's an entity out there has consumed my entire universe. It can't be stopped by any conventional means. It can't be communicated with. It seems to have no real motivations or desires. It simply *is*. I don't think, even if we had the time, we could ever understand it. It's something that exists outside of our current definitions of reality."

"It's not a god either."

"Then maybe it's the devil," Savina mused. "At this point is there a difference?"

"I don't think God wants to consume all of reality and I don't think the Devil has that much of an appetite."

"Then if Steve's not a god, what is he?"

Now it was Mitchell's turn to shrug. "Just another entity we don't understand yet. Just like the Unity."

"Maybe they're just two sides of the same coin," Savina said. "I can't tell you why the Hawia is doing any of this and you can't tell me why Steve sent you here."

"I don't think Steve can tell me why he sent me here," Mitchell said.

"Then maybe he's just not a very good god," Savina replied. "After all, he hasn't done anything to save my universe." She tightened her grip around her cup. "Tell me, what's your universe like?"

Mitchell watched her, trying to catch her gaze, but she refused to meet his eyes. "Not bad," he said. "It's got its high points and its low. Same as any other universe, I suppose."

"You mean there's more? I'm just getting used to the idea of there being two."

"As it's been explained to me, there's quite a few of them."

"Ten?"

"Let's just say I don't think it's possible to count."

Savina exhaled, her cheeks puffing out. "That's… almost as bad as staring into the Hawia. It just goes on forever."

"Eternity is only a bad thing if you get bored easily," Mitchell said.

She laughed at that. But it was an empty, hollow laugh. "You have the Planetary Union in your universe?"

"United Planetary Alliance."

"I like your name better. Planetary Union always gave me a mental image of two planets getting married." She paused and looked up at him. "Is that a thing where you come from? Marriage? Weddings?"

"Yeah, it's a thing."

She nodded, chewing on her lip as she studied him, still without meeting his gaze. "You've been married, haven't you?"

"Twice."

"What happened?"

"Didn't work out."

"So who messed it up? You or them?"

Mitchell didn't answer.

"So, you then," Savina said.

"It was complicated."

"Sounds like our universes aren't that different. Other than the fact that mine's dead and yours isn't." She tried to hide the bitterness in her voice and failed.

"What happened today?" Mitchell asked.

Savina cleared her throat. "We had a breach in our field. It had to be sealed off immediately. If it wasn't, we could put the entire settlement at risk."

"That doesn't explain a whole lot," Mitchell said.

She looked up at him sharply. "Sixteen people just died because of my decision. It's not something I feel like doing a post-mortem on right now."

"I get that," Mitchell said. "It's never easy being the one who has to make all the hard decisions. But that's the job."

"You send a lot of people to their death, Gavin?"

"Too many," he replied. "Doesn't get any easier."

"But it can get a lot harder." She finally met his gaze, the steel returning to her eyes. "An hour ago, there was one hundred and seventy-five of us. Now there's only one hundred and fifty-nine. Every time we lose somebody, we're literally losing a part of our past and what's left of our future."

"But you're still here," Mitchell said. "Fifty years after the end of the universe and you're still here."

"Sure," she agreed hollowly.

"How?" Mitchell asked.

"What?"

"How are you still here?"

"You haven't discovered this yet? Quantum sound vibrations?"

He shook his head.

"Well, maybe this can give you a leg up if you manage to make it back home." She paused to take a breath. "We learned about it far too late for it to do any real good. The Hawia can't move through these quantum sound vibrations. At least, not at first," she said. "It takes them time to match it, the vibration. Once they matched it, it then becomes a part of them. They consume it as they consume anything else. Planets, ships, stars." She shrugged. "And once that happens, there's nothing blocking them."

"Except you're all still here," Mitchell said.

She nodded. "So the generators that produce the vibrations are connected to the computers you saw earlier. Those computers cycle through the variations of quantum vibration signatures, changing them every three minutes. There are billions of variations. Or, at least that's what I've been told. I'm sure you've noticed; the computers are ancient. But there's literally nothing else for them to do. We don't operate any other technology here. It's not safe."

"Why not?"

She stared at him, confused. "Because that's how the Hawia infected us in the first place. Through our technology. Anything with a microchip, a motherboard, a processor, we didn't allow any of it into Apaka. Everything else here is mechanical. This isn't how it happened in your universe?"

Mitchell rubbed the side of his face. "Not exactly."

"Well," she said with a deep sigh. "That's how it happened here. At first, we thought they were limited to our tech. A biomechanical virus, corrupting any piece of technology it came into contact with. A problem for sure, but hardly a sweeping plague upon the universe. It was easily contained. Years went by before we realized that it was appearing independently throughout our universe, without any trail of infection. There was no patient zero spreading it. But again, it was still relatively containable. We had teams in place to step in wherever the virus would appear. We were managing it, until we weren't.

"The Hawia made the jump from our tech to, well, everything else basically overnight. They bled through our technology, infecting and consuming everyone they came into contact with. And then, of course, they would spread across the planet's surface. I don't know what held them back for so long. Nobody really does. We didn't have the time or the resources to examine any of it and by the time the Hawia had figured out how to move from our tech to us, it was too late for us to do anything but run." She swallowed, holding back her emotions. "If you try to be objective about, it's a rather effective way of destroying a species."

"How late did you discover the quantum shield?" Mitchell asked.

"Too late," she replied. "It has one fatal flaw in its design: There's no sound in space. Of course, that's not a problem anymore. Because there's no space in space now. It's just the Hawia."

"There has to be others," he said.

"Maybe," she conceded. "But even if there were, how could we find them? The Hawia eat signals as much as they eat everything else. When you think about it, it's kind of a miracle we've lasted as long as we have." She raised both eyebrows. "Maybe that's why Steve sent you here."

"For your technology?" he asked.

"To remind you that miracles are still possible," she said.

"I haven't known Steve for very long, but I can safely say that doesn't sound like him."

Savina let go of her cup and reached across the table, taking his hand in hers. Mitchell was momentarily surprised by the gesture and then he was surprised at how soft her hand felt.

"What are you going to do?" she asked. "You don't know how you got here. You don't know how to get back. What are you going to do?"

Mitchell looked at her hand, clasped around his, and then met her gaze. "What am I allowed to do?"

"You're not our prisoner, Gavin," she replied. "You're not even our guest. You're just here at the end of the universe like the rest of us."

"I have a ship," Mitchell said. "A crew. I need to know what's happened to them."

"And how are you going to do that?" Savina asked. "I don't have a spare universe-to-universe communicator laying around."

Mitchell pulled his hand from hers, thinking about the ancient computers. "What happens when the generators go?"

She sat back. If she was upset by his rejection, she didn't show it. Or, at least, she didn't give it any special attention beyond the multitude of other emotions she was feeling. "There are three redundant generators for each primary."

Mitchell ran the numbers in his head. They weren't getting replacement parts around here. Once something broke down, they didn't have any way of replacing it.

"And when they all fail?"

Savina placed her hands on the table, palms up. "Then I guess that's the end. It's not that much of a twist ending. After all, look what they've done to the rest of the universe."

"How many times has it happened already?" Mitchell asked. "How many times has the scene from earlier already played out?"

"Twice before," she answered quietly.

"How the hell are you doing this?" Mitchell asked, his voice dropping to match hers.

Savina's shoulders slumped. "I honestly don't know anymore. I just don't know."

A new alarm started blaring.

She jerked upright, jumping out of her seat. "No…"

Around them the asteroid shook violently.

"What's going on?" Mitchell asked. "Is it another generator?"

Savina didn't bother answering. She started running for the command center.

A shockwave rippled through the asteroid and the ceiling cracked and broke, raining down on the promenade.

Mitchell jumped back, raising an arm to shield his face.

All around him people screamed as their home violently shook, threatening to crack apart at the very seams.

And then everything came to a stop.

But that was underselling it.

Mitchell gripped the back of the chair for support. The space around him hung at a thirty-five-degree angle as Apaka abruptly stopped shaking.

People were frozen in mid-step. Some had their arms flailing in the air. Some were even in the process of tripping and falling. But they were all the same regardless: frozen.

Falling debris just hung in the air, as if it were trapped in some invisible amber.

Sound was muted, as though someone had thrown an insanely thick blanket on top of every noise. He could still hear everything, but it sounded flat, distant and dull.

Even the air itself felt different, almost thicker. Mitchell found himself slightly struggling to inhale.

"What the hell?" Mitchell gasped.

A singularly calm and rather bemused voice spoke up behind him. "Don't you wish you had just taken the easy way now?"

Mitchell turned and saw Steve standing there.

27

USS DEFIANCE

THERE WAS a voice in Calloway's head, and she was almost certain that it wasn't hers. She was very familiar with all the little voices that took up residence in her mind: her doubts, her insecurities, her fears, her running mental commentary on her crewmates, and this voice was definitely not one of those.

She tried her best to ignore it. To shove it to the back of her mind, to drown it out, but the voice would not listen. It would not go away. If anything, it grew more insistent with every effort she made to silence it.

Calloway sat on her small bed, her knees drawn up to her chin and her arms wrapped around her shins, trying her best to not think about the voice, or anything else that had happened to her that didn't make any sense.

Of course, the moment she tried not to think about it, it was all she could think about.

What had she been doing in Cargo Bay Two? She didn't know.

That wasn't true. She didn't *want* to know. There was a difference and she had to acknowledge the difference.

Because ignorance was bliss. Ignorance meant that if she didn't know about it, she couldn't be held responsible for it.

But when she had stepped into sickbay with Zemble, that voice that had previously been a quiet whisper at the back of her head, transformed into a damn megaphone. Now she couldn't stop hearing it.

The Voice wanted things. It wanted her to do things. It poked around the edge of her conscious mind with little mental talons. She imagined she could feel it stabbing at her mind, trying to get a reaction that would result in something it desired.

The voice that wasn't her own didn't want her to stay in her quarters.

Calloway tried to keep her gaze focused on the wall in front of her bed, but she kept finding her eyes drifting to the door. Sometimes she wouldn't realize it had happened until after she had been staring at the door for almost a full minute. Calloway would quickly tear her gaze away from the door and focus it back on the wall.

But the Voice *pushed* at her.

She couldn't feel it in her muscles yet. She didn't have the sensation of her limbs taking commands from someone, something, other than her own conscious mind. But she knew that couldn't be far away.

Calloway needed to talk to somebody. But who could she talk to? Who wouldn't think she was just losing her mind?

In sickbay, Zemble had seen *something*. So had Dheer.

But here she was, in her quarters. Not in sickbay, not in the brig, not even tied up in a damn straitjacket. She was just confined to her quarters. House arrest. Actually, maybe not even that. She had no idea if Zemble had posted a security officer outside her door. She should get up and check.

Calloway started moving before she realized what had happened. Her feet were off the bed and she was nearly standing before she caught herself.

That wasn't *her*.

That *notion*. That *idea*. That *thought*. It hadn't belonged to her.

Calloway pulled her legs back to her chest and wrapped her arms around them again. This time, so tight she could feel her arms almost hurting from the strain.

She wanted to close her eyes, but she knew that would only make it worse. It would make her feel closed off and alone with the Voice. It would make the Voice feel larger than it really was. And it was already big enough. If it got any bigger…

A terrifying thought occurred to her and she tried her best to push it away, to ignore it.

She was Erin Calloway. No more, no less. Her body, her mind, belonged to her and no one else.

Nothing would take her mind. Not even a strange voice that didn't belong.

Calloway shuddered and tightened her grip around her legs. She needed something to distract her from the voice in her head.

"Computer." She jumped slightly at the sound of her voice. The silence in her room had grown deafening. And in the absence of anything else, she had almost forgotten what her own voice sounded like.

No, she thought, that was a crazy thought. Don't be crazy. Right now, no crazy thoughts allowed.

Calloway swallowed and spoke again, her voice cracking slightly, "Computer, play music list: Calloway Heavy Metal."

There was a soft chirp of the computer acknowledging and a moment later her quarters were filled with the screeching noise of an electric guitar and a man screaming into a microphone, reminding his son to include everyone in his prayers.

For the briefest of seconds, Calloway almost felt a sense of relief as the Voice was drowned out over the blasting music.

But then the Voice just grew louder.

28

"WHAT IN THE blue blazes of Xoqnin's inflamed anus are you idiots doing up here?" Warrick shouted, barging into sickbay. "I don't know if you've heard, but I'm trying to keep this damn ship from *coming apart at the seams.* And just when I think I don't have enough to deal with, every console down in engineering starts screaming that you've got some power surge going on up here that's going tear *another hole in the damn hull.* I can one hundred percent guarantee you that our structural integrity sure as hell is not going to hold if that happens. This old bird was built to take a lot, but having whole chunks of it ripped out of it all willy-nilly *literally* its breaking point So, who wants to fess up around here?"

Warrick was halfway through sickbay, shouting at the top of his lungs before he realized that nobody was paying any attention to him. Instead, they were all focused on Keane, who was standing buck naked and without so much as a scratch on him.

Warrick came to an abrupt stop and joined the rest of sickbay in staring dumbfoundedly at Keane.

"The hell?" Warrick muttered.

"That's certainly one way of putting it." Keane coughed into one hand while he tried to cover himself up with his other.

No one in sickbay said anything. Nobody had even really heard Warrick's rant. They all just stared at Keane, who was very, very naked.

The nurse with the echoing voice let out a long trailing, "Ooooh," as her hand fluttered to her chest.

Keane looked around the group of the people staring at him. While none of them made eye contact with him, they weren't necessarily avoiding his gaze. They were just…staring in shock. He tried to find an empty console or bed to step behind, but nothing jumped out at him. As casually as he could Keane lowered his other hand down so both were covering his crotch. "This is, uh, starting to feel a little awkward."

A green haired woman stepped out from behind Keane, looking around at the shocked and confused members of the *Defiance* crew. "Did I do something wrong?"

Keane jumped a little bit, not realizing there was anybody behind him. "Who the hell are you?"

Rabkin stepped up next to Sadler and said out of the corner of his mouth, "You should probably do something."

"Sure, sure," Sadler said. She sounded vaguely numb with shock. "But, counterpoint, sickbay's really your domain."

Dheer stepped up to Keane, examining his left arm, looking for some sign of a seam or artificial connection. She pressed her fingers against the muscles of his shoulder, tracing their outlines and then digging in until she pressed against bone.

"Okay, um, this is actually getting weirder." Keane

tried to take a step back and bumped into the green haired woman. He glanced back at her again. "Do I, uh, know you?"

"No," she replied.

"Okay, well, hi. I'm Keane. Normally I'm wearing clothes." Keane said.

"In order to pronounce my name, you would most likely suffer some kind of permanent brain damage. An aneurysm, perhaps? Your crewmates have agreed to call me Sharon."

Keane nodding, swallowing. "Ah, well, it's nice to meet you, Sharon. I think?" He turned back to Dheer, who still hadn't said a word. Her gaze was focused on his body, searching for something. "Can somebody get me some clothes before, I don't know, we get to the point where none of us is going to be able to make eye contact later? And, also, maybe somebody can fill me in on what's going on? Because the last thing I remember was that I was about to die painfully. Also, I'm pretty sure I was missing a limb."

"Yes," the green haired woman said. "Your body was in a very poor condition."

"That's the understatement of the year," Rabkin said under his breath.

Dheer grabbed Keane by the shoulders and turned him around so that he was face to face with the green haired lady.

"Oh," Keane said awkwardly, bumping into her. "Hi, again."

"I don't believe this," Dheer whispered.

"Not going to lie, that's the first time I've heard anyone say that about my butt," Keane said. He gave the green haired woman an awkward, uneven smile. "That's supposed to be a joke. To, you know, lighten the mood."

The green haired woman arched an eyebrow. She ran her gaze down the length of his body and then back to his eyes. "Because this is uncomfortable?"

Keane blinked, avoiding direct eye contact with her. "Yeah, sure, a little bit."

"It's understandable," she replied. "You're not exactly an impressive species."

Keane swallowed nervously. "Okay, well, that didn't really help."

Dheer pressed her hand between his shoulder blades and then worked their way down to his left leg.

Keane jumped a little and took three giant steps back from everyone, holding one hand over his crotch and the other one palm out to hold anyone else back. "Seriously, what the hell is going on here? And maybe somebody can answer that while they give me some *damn clothes.*"

A jumpsuit suddenly smacked him in the face.

"Thank you," Keane said.

"Don't mention it," Rabkin replied. "Miracle recovery or not, I really don't need to see your naked ass prancing around here." He turned to the green haired woman. "What the hell did you do."

"I think it should be obvious," she replied. "I fixed him. I believe the proper response in this type of scenario is 'Thank you.' To which I would reply, 'You are welcome.'"

Nobody said anything as Keane quickly pulled on the jumpsuit.

The green haired woman frowned. "You are welcome, then."

"This doesn't make any sense," Dheer said. She grabbed Keane, pushing him onto an exam table.

"Hey," he said, barely having time to finish zipping up.

"You can't do this," Dheer said. She moved over to the

nearest diagnostic console and started pulling up fresh data on Keane.

"You seem upset by the results," the green haired woman said.

Dheer whirled around on her and pointed at Keane. "That man was missing an arm, over six pints of blood and was looking at the very real possibility of permanent brain damage, assuming he wasn't completely consumed by the Unity infection." There was a soft beep behind her from the console. She turned back around to read the results. "This isn't possible."

"I'm not complaining," Keane said, holding up both hands. "I'm mostly just a little confused and even more embarrassed. Last time this many people saw me naked I was in a regeneration tank being studied by the doctors at Jupiter Med for the best way to replace forty-seven percent of my internal organs."

Dheer turned to him, her face numb with shock. "It's not just your Unity injuries, Cayden."

"I'm sorry? What's that supposed to mean?"

She moved so he could see the data on the console. "All of your internal organs have been restored. There's no sign of your injuries from Serenity Base."

Keane stared at the screen for a second and then down at his abdomen. He placed both hands on his stomach and pressed, not entirely certain what he was supposed to feel. The replacements had felt mostly normal. Or, at least, after thirteen years they felt normal. So…

He looked back up at the screen, as though maybe Dheer was playing some kind of trick on him.

Keane took a deep breath. It felt different. It felt…

He looked at the green haired woman.

"Who the hell are you?"

29

SHARON SET the green ball down on the table with a soft *clink*. She looked up to address Sadler and Rabkin. "You cannot possibly understand the significance of this."

They stood in Rabkin's office just off the center of sickbay.

"Well, I mean, I've seen paperweights before," Rabkin said. "So, there's that."

Sharon was unamused. "You attempt to make light of what you don't understand."

"Oh, if we're going to talk about things I don't understand, why don't we start with what you did to Keane out there."

"As I explained already, I fixed him."

"You *fixed* him?" Rabkin shook his head. "You did a *hell* of a lot more than *that*. He was missing *body parts*. He was *dying*. Despite whatever crazy thing Dheer wanted to do, he wasn't going to survive. Because nobody survives when they get attacked by the damn Unity."

Sharon frowned. "You want me to explain."

"Hell, yes!"

"And how would you suggest I do that?" she asked. "How you would suggest I take concepts that to me, are as simple as colors to you, and explain them to you? How would you explain the notion of language to a species who cannot speak, cannot see, cannot hear and doesn't understand there's a larger world beyond the cave they are stuck in?"

Rabkin folded his arms. "For starters, I'd probably speak real slowly."

"Your crewman is well again. Be happy for him," she said. "It is not every day someone escapes the clutches of the Unity."

Rabkin opened his mouth with the intent to continue the argument, but Sadler cut him off with a wave of her hand.

"Let it go," Sadler said.

Rabkin shot her a look. "You pick a hell of a time to decide you want to be in charge."

Sharon pointed to the ball on the table. "This is, as you call it, the Unity. I should not have been able to extract it from your crewman. To put it as simply as possible, you're not supposed to do this to it."

Sadler and Rabkin looked at each other, confused.

"Okay, what are you supposed to do to it?" Sadler asked.

"Nothing," she replied. "As I'm sure my brother has already explained to you, the Unity are an unstoppable force. You don't do anything to them. At best, you can strive to stay out of their way. However, their path will eventually, inevitably, intersect with yours. There's nothing you can do about that. And when that time inevitably comes, there's nothing you can do to stop them. Struggling will not matter. Running will not help. You will simply be consumed, as every dimension before yours has."

"Like we don't have enough to worry about with you people dropping in with your damn Debbie Downer updates," Rabkin grumbled.

"I'm sorry if you find this news disturbing," Sharon said. "From my point of view, it's simply a statement of facts. As you would explain how the reproductive process works, I explain to you how the Unification works."

"Except…" Sadler gestured at the green ball.

Sharon looked down at it, her head tilted to the side. "Yes. Except for this." She dropped down, squatting back low enough until she was eye-level with the ball. "I was not expecting this."

"At the risk of the obvious question, what were you expecting?" Sadler asked.

Sharon straightened up. "My singular goal upon arriving here was to clean up any mess my brother may have made." She looked up at them. "Steve believes he's helping, blissfully unaware that often his help tends to create more problems for those he seeks to help."

"Blissfully unaware?" Rabkin repeated dubiously.

Sharon picked up the ball, turning it over in her hands as if it weighed next to nothing. "He's family. We all want to see the best in family. I believe that is a constant across the dimensions."

"That's nice to hear," Rabkin said. "I was worried that the sense of family was something you people from a higher dimension wouldn't understand."

"We also understand sarcasm," she said, not looking up.

Sadler looked at him sideways. Rabkin avoided her gaze.

"The *Eternal Hand of God* was my brother's…pet project?" She paused and looked at them with a raised eyebrow. "Am I using that phrase correctly?"

"Depends on how the rest of your story goes," Rabkin said.

"Steve followed the *Eternal Hand of God* as it made its way up through the Stack. Using it as a litmus for a representative of each dimension. Inevitably, they would fail the test. Much like I assumed you would have."

"Maybe it would have helped if we knew we were being tested," Sadler said.

Sharon regarded her with a steady, yet dull expression. "It's been my experience that all of life is an ongoing test."

"Great," Rabkin said. "On top of everything else, you're a first year philosophy student."

"Wait," Sadler said. "You said you assumed we would have failed the test."

Sharon nodded. "Yes I did. I do not suffer from any short-term memory issues."

"Does that mean we didn't fail?" Sadler asked.

Sharon raised both eyebrows, pursing her lips before she spoke. "That has yet to be determined."

"What the hell is that supposed to mean?" Rabkin asked.

"Simply that the *Eternal Hand of God* has never been destroyed before now," Sharon said. "And even more relevant, my brother has never absconded with a member of another dimension until he took your captain."

"Wonderful," Rabkin grumbled. "We're raking up all kinds of firsts left and right here. It's going to look real great on our universal tombstone."

Sharon seemed to not hear him, or purposely chose to ignore him. "The better question," she continued, "is what was wrong with the Unity on the *Eternal Hand of God?*"

"What was wrong with it?" Sadler echoed.

Sharon gestured towards the ball. "Clearly something

was wrong. Otherwise I shouldn't have been able to fix your crewman. It was sick."

"Sick?" Rabkin asked. "What the hell does that mean?"

"Did I not use the correct word?" she asked. "This member of the Unity was not well. Does the word 'sick' not mean the same thing?"

"Sure it does," Rabkin said. "So, what? It had a cold? A fever blister? Maybe a bad case of the runs?"

"I don't know its specific diagnosis," Sharon said. "It is…difficult to study the Unity. Impossible, really. What it was sick with, I have no idea and will probably never know."

"If any of this is supposed to be helpful, maybe one of us needs to explain what that word means," Rabkin said impatiently.

"I'm sorry," Sharon replied. "I haven't made myself clear." She looked at both of them. "The Unity doesn't get sick. Not once. Not ever. It does not happen."

30

"I FEEL *AMAZING*," Keane said, making a fist with a hand that hadn't been there a few hours ago.

"You shouldn't," Dheer said.

He grinned at her. "I feel like I could wrestle a damn Kracux."

She didn't look up from her console. They were situated in a private exam room away from the prying eyes of literally everyone in sickbay who had just seen a nearly dead man completely healed and restored in the blink of an eye.

"Do you know what a Kracux is?" he asked her.

"Yes," Dheer replied, clearly not paying any attention to him.

He held out his arms as wide as they went. "They're three times my size. Extremely vicious. Claws that are nearly three inches long and they excrete a numbing venom, but they don't use it. They're considered one of the most highly intelligent animals in the galaxy. They don't build anything. They don't have any obvious signs of communication. They don't give a flying fuck about fire.

They are just pure savage killing machines. Even Zemble would think twice about getting into a dust up with one and I feel like I could take on *two* right now. No weapons. Straight up hand to, well, claw, I guess, combat." He nodded enthusiastically. "That's pretty impressive."

Dheer finally looked at him. "If by impressive you mean that you just barely escaped death and you're already looking for a new way to get yourself needlessly killed, I completely agree with you."

He held out his hands. "I'm just trying to explain to you how amazing I feel."

"I want you to understand that you shouldn't," she said. "What you're feeling right now? It's an endorphin rush. According to these readings, you're on a high that's equivalent to a Backlon spice junkie."

He looked at her dubiously. "Am I supposed to be feeling guilty about this? Because, I'll be honest with you. Sure, the whole I'm missing forty-seven percent of my original internal organs thing was a great pickup line and it was great for winning all the drinking games, but if I had to choose, I'd much rather have all of my original parts."

Dheer tapped at the screen. There was an outline of Keane's body, broken down layer by layer. "Except these aren't your original parts."

"They feel pretty original to me," Keane said.

Dheer pulled up another file and positioned it side-by-side with Keane's current scans. "These are from your last exam. This is from today."

Keane looked back and forth between them and shrugged. "Okay. Well, I'm a security specialist, not a doctor. So you might as well be showing me ancient Uboklu medical scripts."

Dheer rolled her eyes. "Let's ignore the big things."

Keane again looked at the arm that shouldn't be there.

"Alright, but it feels like we're purposely ignoring the best part about all this."

Dheer ignored him and started pointing things out. "You had six scars located on your right hip that predated the accident on Serenity Base."

Keane nodded. "Yeah. They were from a skiing accident on Meputurn when I was sixteen. I misjudged the distance on a jump and ended up impaled on three branches of a Merkli'n tree. The impalement wasn't too bad, you know, as impalements went. But the sap from a Merkli'n tree is basically like liquid fire to human skin. Burned me like a son of a bitch."

Dheer grabbed his face and directed it to his current scans. "Those scars are no longer there."

Keane blinked. "What?"

"They're gone," she said. "Along with all the scar tissue, the burn scars and the history of the broken bones. Also? You had your wisdom teeth extracted when you were eighteen?"

Keane nodded, a vague numbness settling in over him.

"They're back."

"They're…back?"

She nodded.

"That's not supposed to happen is it?" Keane asked. "They don't grow back."

"Not for humans and last time I checked, you're not a Phulkin."

Keane reached into his mouth, not sure what he expected to find and immediately found something unexpected.

Dheer watched him and slowly nodded. "You had three teeth replaced two years ago."

Keane pulled his hand out. "They got knocked out

during a bar fight on Starbase *Niagara* with an Elwat who was a little less agreeable than Zemble is."

"They're back, too."

Keane didn't say anything for a moment. He just sat there on the exam bed, letting all the information wash over him.

"So, it's not just my recent injuries or even my extreme ones," he said.

"It's every part of you that was broken or replaced since the moment you were born. In fact, according to this," she pointed to the current scan. "The computer thinks you're essentially the perfect specimen of a twenty-five-year-old man."

Keane smiled at that crookedly.

Dheer wasn't amused. "The *computer* thinks that," she reminded. "According to the birthdate on your file, you're still thirty-five."

"Okay." Keane's head bobbed up and down. "This is still a good thing."

"I didn't say it wasn't."

"I mean, you're certainly casting it in a creepy and disturbing light," Keane said. "Half the human race would love to be in my position right now."

"Except we don't know what your position is."

Keane hopped off the bed.

"Where do you think you're going?" Dheer asked him.

"I need to get back to work."

She shook her head and pointed back to the bed. "You're not going anywhere."

"You literally just said I'm in the best health I've ever been."

"At what cost?"

"Excuse me?"

"We have no idea what kind of effect this is going to have on your mental wellbeing," she said.

"Well, if I had to hazard a guess, it's going to be a pretty good effect."

"You know a lot of Backlon spice addicts that end up having healthy productive lives? Because I don't. Most of them end up dead due to a severe judgment impairment that leaves them feeling invincible."

Keane held up a hand that had been previously forcibly torn from his body and pointed to it. "I was pretty sure that if I made it off that ship, this was going to be a prosthetic for the rest of my life. It's not. So maybe feeling a little invincible isn't the worst thing in the world right now."

He started for the door and Dheer jumped in front of him.

"Except you're *not* invincible," she said. "Some entity from a dimension we don't understand happened to show up and stitch you back together in a way we don't understand."

"Everything feels like it's in the right place." Keane gestured at the console. "You see anything on there that suggests that my hip bone isn't connected to my thigh bone?"

Dheer gave him a withering glare. "That doesn't mean it's a good thing."

"Doesn't mean it's a bad thing, either."

"And what happens when something goes wrong and this über powerful entity isn't around to stitch you up again?" Dheer asked.

"I still have the utmost confidence in your abilities," he replied, stepping around her.

"Well, I don't," she said and that stopped him cold. "Because I don't know how she did what she did. I don't know if it can be duplicated. And, worst of all, I don't know if it's compatible with any of our less-than-miraculous medical techniques. What happens if you get shot by a fusion rifle and what's normally a standard procedure, assuming nothing vital was hit, becomes a critical condition when your body doesn't respond to any of the treatment because it's not functioning the way it's intended to?"

Keane didn't answer for a second. He just looked at her, watching Dheer moved from deeply concerned physician to frightened friend. He opened his mouth, unsure what he was going to say, but wanting to say something helpful. But in the end, he just shrugged. "I guess that's just life, Marlize."

Keane stepped out of the exam room and Dheer pounded the console in frustration.

31

"You're looking pretty spry for a man who's supposed to be dead before the day's out," Zemble said as Keane stepped out of sickbay.

Keane fidgeted with the collar of his uniform. "It's all those vitamins you make fun of me for taking."

Zemble fell in step beside him as they made their way down the corridor. "The limp's gone, too?"

"I got a complete makeover," Keane said. "New coat of paint, too."

Zemble frowned. "That's a shame."

"Oh?"

"I was starting to like the limp," he said. "It gave you some character."

Keane rolled his eyes, tugging at the collar again. "You know what my favorite character trait is? Being your superior officer."

"You say that like it's supposed to mean something," Zemble said. "But in your absence, you'll notice that I managed to keep the ship from being overrun by any space pirates."

"What about the green haired lady that stitched me back together?" Keane said.

"Clearly she was here to do the Lord's work," Zemble replied with a straight face.

Keane groaned. "Come on…"

"I'm not joking."

"I know. That's what makes it worse." Keane made a face and yanked on the collar. Finally he just lowered the zipper a full inch and exhaled a relieved sigh.

"What's the matter?" Zemble asked.

"Felt like the stupid collar kept choking me. Couldn't get it to feel right."

"Interesting," Zemble said.

"Why?"

"I don't know," he admitted. "Just seemed like something that seemed interesting."

"The green haired lady?" Keane said, bringing them back on topic.

"It seemed rude to throw her in the brig once she pulled you back from the brink of death."

"At the very least you could have questioned her," Keane said.

"Sure, but again, it seemed rude."

"Rude?"

"Besides, Commander Sadler seems on top of it."

"And you want my job?"

"Actually, no I don't," Zemble said. "I don't know if anybody told you, but I experienced my own traumatic incident while you were off exploring your derelict death trap. Being in charge really cut into my recovery time. I need to process what happened to me."

"What happened to you?"

"I got sent to some alternate dimension where time had

no meaning and I was unable to breathe for what felt like eternity," Zemble said. "Among other things."

Keane stopped abruptly. "Seriously?"

"It seems like it would make for a poor joke," Zemble said.

"Shit," Keane breathed. "What else did I miss?"

"Calloway had a reaction."

Keane's eyes narrowed. "What kind of reaction?"

Zemble quickly ran down what happened once he found her in Cargo Bay Two and brought her up to sickbay.

Keane frowned. "Where is she now?"

"Confined to quarters."

"You've really got a thing against the brig, don't you?"

Zemble shrugged his massive shoulders. "I don't like throwing friends in there."

"Are we sure Sharon's our friend?"

"Her brother sent me away to an alternate dimension to be tortured for all eternity. She healed you, bringing you back from the literal brink of death. At very least, I'm willing to consider her a friendly acquaintance."

Keane rolled up his sleeves. "Come on, let's go check on Calloway. You can catch me up on everything else on the way."

32

"Perhaps it would be beneficial for you to see the larger picture of reality." Sharon pressed her fingertips together as she stood in front of Sadler and Rabkin. Between them, the green ball sat on the table like an unspeaking fourth participant.

"I'm too old for mind altering drugs," Rabkin said. "Reality's enough of a pain in the butt for me."

Sharon pressed her lips together distastefully. "I am speaking of the Unity. More specifically, the nature of their origins."

Sadler and Rabkin looked at each other surprise.

Sharon paused, letting her gaze drift between them for a moment. "I presume my brother did not take the opportunity to share this with you?"

"He gave us the campfire story," Rabkin said.

"Of course he did." She sighed. "He fancies himself the eternal teacher, but rarely does he have the patience to truly teach anything."

"That's a real polite way of saying your brother is an impatient asshole," Rabkin said.

Sharon ignored him. "There was a...member of my species. As with Steve and I, it is nearly impossible to tell you his true name. So let's call him..." she paused for a moment, thinking it over. "Let's call him *Gary*."

"Gary?" Sadler repeated.

Sharon nodded. "Yes. That sounds like the name of an individual who'd damn the multiverse in an incidental sort of way in his pursuit of knowledge."

"Oh, this sounds like it's going to be a fun story." Rabkin sat down. "Better get comfortable."

For what felt like a long minute, Sharon didn't speak. She stared down at the green ball on the desk, as though expecting, waiting, for it to contribute something. Or perhaps stop her. Then, almost abruptly, she snapped her gaze up from the ball back to Rabkin and Sadler.

"It is an undisputed fact that...Gary was one of our greatest." Sharon held her hands out, her fingers slightly bent at the knuckle. "A genius among geniuses. This is not speculation. I understand that you have no reason to believe me, of course. But it is true. Or *was*, at the very least.

"But more than just being a genius, Gary believed that there was truly no end to one's education. Despite everything at our fingertips and believe me when I say that we had a multiverse of opportunities and options available to us, Gary believed there was still *more*.

"He had a thirst for knowledge that could simply not be quenched because he *believed* it could not be. And, truth be told, it was an admirable trait. Until it became his undoing.

"As I am sure Steve has already explained to you, because this is the part he never bores of, this dimension is but one of many. They are stacked upon each other, stretching out into infinity and into the abyss. My people are from the top of the Stack.

"The Unity is from the Abyss."

Sharon paused, her gaze darkening for a moment.

"The Unity *is* the Abyss.

"Time at our end of the Stack measures differently than it does for you," she continued. "So when I say that Gary spent millennia traveling different dimensions of the Stack, understand I am speaking both literally and figuratively. He was fascinated by all of the lower dimensions and he was equally fascinated by how far we can go. My people travel the Stack through what we call the Network. To you, it appears as a fourth-dimensional spacial distortion known as a wormhole. For us, it is a path through unlimited possibilities.

"But like all paths, it comes to an end. Because, as I'm sure you understand even here in this dimension, there is no path to the Abyss. Nor should there be. Because, after all, it is the Abyss.

"Gary, in his infinite quest for knowledge, asked: why? Why was there no path to the Abyss? Why could our Network not breach this mysterious barrier at the bottom of the Stack? And why weren't we more curious about what lay beyond in the Abyss?

"My people argued that it was the Abyss. There was nothing in the Abyss. There was nothing to be gained from the Abyss. There was nothing to be seen in the Abyss. It was a fool's errand to seek anything from the Abyss, because it was the *Abyss*.

"Gary did not subscribe to this philosophy. More than that, he spoke out against it. He said it was *backwards*. It was *ill-conceived*. It was *less* of us. He was mocked and ridiculed for this.

"In the end, Gary stepped away from us. Disappearing

into his laboratories for untold millennia, determined to prove us all wrong. He would find value in the Abyss. He would find purpose in the Abyss. He would find untold sources of knowledge in the Abyss. He would find a way to the Abyss.

"And he did.

"And the Unity was there to greet him."

Sharon stopped. She lowered her head.

Sadler and Rabkin were speechless. How much time had passed since she had started talking? Neither of them knew. Something in her voice pulled them away, deeper into a story that was unraveling faster than they could absorb it.

Suddenly, Sharon's gaze snapped back up.

"What happened next should sound familiar," she continued. "Because it is the same encounter any species has with the Unity.

"Upon breaching the barrier between the lower stacks and the Abyss, Gary was lost to us. Consumed, absorbed into the Unity. His essence, his life force, his being, his *knowledge*.

"We do not know what the Unity was before Gary made contact with it. It is impossible to know. All that is known was what the Unity became *after* Gary was consumed."

Sharon gestured to Sadler and Rabkin. "Despite your primitive nature, your sensors have undoubtedly detected the Network. Perhaps some of you have even discovered ways of using it to traverse distances here in your own dimension. But imagine handing one of your computers to a child from your distant past. They discover how to adjust colors on it, turn it on and off. Perhaps even play a game with it. They don't understand the computer's full potential. They lack the ability to understand it. As you do with the Network.

"The Unity, however, took everything that Gary was, and this included his knowledge, which included the intimate details of how he pierced the barriers of the Abyss and how the Network works.

"This could not stand. Obviously. Knowledge is power. And in this instance, this was a power that belonged to no one but us.

"In our attempt to fix what Gary had broken, we foolishly sent more of our people down into the Abyss to curb, to *tame*, to *control* the Unity.

"But the Unity is the Abyss. And you cannot control the Abyss. You cannot do anything to the Abyss. That was a lesson that was…*difficult* for my people to learn."

Sharon took a deep breath. "There were so many of us. Not as many as the multitude of species that populate these lower dimensions, but we were a plentiful species.

"Now there are less than ten of us left.

"Ten. We kept sending people down there, hoping to save the others, hoping to stop the Abyss. Or, perhaps, more accurately, we did it out of our foolish pride. Because what could destroy us? What species from the lower stacks could even conceive of a method to kill something that they would have considered a *god*?

"And yet, there are only ten of us left.

"In the end, out of desperation, we decided to break the direct connection with the Abyss. We could not let it gain access to our dimension. It would be…*catastrophic*. The Unity had taken almost all of us, but there was still much left in our dimension that it could consume, and we dare not lose what little we had left. So we did the next best thing and closed off our dimension, our home.

"The ten of us scattered ourselves among the Stack.

We found things to occupy ourselves with. To distract ourselves, really. We were the last of our species and that was something that none of us cared to dwell on. Ultimately, though, our goal was to stay as far away from the Abyss as possible. Which, of course, became more difficult with every passing day.

"The Abyss, the Unity, faced with no other way to gain access to our dimension, and armed with the knowledge of the Network, began its slow march towards Heaven, consuming everything in its path. Because you cannot contain the Abyss. You cannot ignore the Abyss. The Abyss simply *is*."

Sharon drew herself up straight and spread out her arms. "And this, this is the true nature of what you call reality."

33

APAKA 2221

"You know, and I don't say this lightly, but you do rather impress me." Steve sounded almost jovial as he navigated his way around debris frozen in mid-air. He reached out and gently pushed a rock out of his face. He had traded his Fleet Admiral uniform for a simple black suit. The only splash of color was a red dot on the tie that seemed to grow blurrier the closer he got to Mitchell. "There aren't many people who can survive moving through the Stack unprotected. In most cases, a lower life form such as yourself is reduced to...Well, how do I put this delicately." Steve pressed the palms of his hands together and tilted his head side to side. "I believe the technical term is that their brains are turned to jelly." He smirked, as though he had just made a small joke.

Mitchell didn't respond. His focus was split between Steve and the fact that everything was frozen around him. But after Steve had pushed the rock out of his face, Mitchell realized that everything wasn't so much as frozen as it was slowed down. Everything was still in motion, just at a fraction of what would be considered normal speed.

"But you?" Steve continued. "Not only is your mind not a gooey little puddle slowly circling the drain, but you recovered in, well, record time." He paused and then added, "Well, record time considering your handicap as a human being from a lower dimension. To be fair, the Ov'eas, who are just a few dimensions up from you, have been known to traverse the Stack unencumbered, recovering in mere minutes. But that's not something you can really compete with. Still, well done." He clapped his hands lightly. "That's impressive. I'm impressed. You should be impressed, too. Give yourself a little pat on the back. I would do it, but honestly, I'm still not sure if I can catch anything from you humans." He frowned. "I'd hate to end up with a severe case of mediocrity after an existence of brilliance."

Now that he was aware of it, Mitchell could feel the sensation of everything slowing down around him. He wondered if the effect extended to him. Then he wondered if everyone else on Apaka was aware that they had been slowed down.

"Tell me, what did you see as you passed through the thin membranes of unreality that separate your dimensions? It was your ex-wife, wasn't it?" Steve nodded, chuckling. "I know what you're thinking and no, I'm not a mindreader. I don't have to be a mindreader to read you, Mitchell. You might as well be monologuing your motivations and emotional arcs out loud. The word best used to describe you is: transparent. Extremely transparent, actually." Steve clasped his hands behind his back. "But again, I have to say, I am impressed. You found yourself face to face with the love of your life, or at least someone or something roughly approximately whatever the chemical misfires in that tiny brain of yours characterize as 'love,' and you turned away from it." He paused.

"Well, I suppose 'impressive' may not be the correct word. You could have been doing something right, under stupid reasoning. Which, if we're being honest, is more your species M.O." Steve stopped and frowned at Mitchell.

"Hello?" Steve snapped his fingers in Mitchell's face. He stood directly in front of him now. "Are you paying attention? I'm trying to pay you a compliment. If you're not going to listen, I'm not going to waste my time. You don't know this about me, but I only hand out compliments once every couple of millennia."

"What the hell is going on?" Mitchell asked.

Steve gestured aimlessly. "That should be fairly self-evident. You've got a front row seat at the end of a universe. Please tell me you're not that dense. I literally just spent a minute complimenting you. I simply cannot deal with that kind of disappointment right now."

Mitchell locked his gaze on Steve. "You took me from my ship."

Steve folded his arms. "You should be thanking me for that. After all, your ship was about to become nothing more than very poorly refined space dust."

Anger flared across Mitchell's face. "My crew is dead?"

Steve cast his gaze up towards the falling ceiling. "Well, that depends on what you consider to be 'alive.' From my point of view, I can hardly consider you to be imbued with the same life force and sense of purpose as I am."

Mitchell lunged for him.

Abruptly, Steve wasn't standing there anymore.

Mitchell lurched forward awkwardly, his body temporarily flailing as it didn't have anything to run into as expected. Then he realized that he wasn't flailing as much as he thought he should be.

Mitchell pulled his arms back and it felt like he was

trying to move through dense air. He turned around to find Steve standing behind him.

"Let's not do that again," Steve said. "It's just going to end badly for you and, honestly, do you really need that kind of headache right now?"

Mitchell's hands balled up into fists, but he didn't move from his new spot. "What the hell happened to my ship?"

"I suppose I'm supposed to think it's admirable that in the midst of all this, your first priority is your crew." Steve made a *tut-tut* sound and shook his head. "It should go without saying, but I don't find it anything save for being rather pathetic. You really need to learn to focus on the here and now. Be in the *moment*, Gavin. Because this *moment* is what it's all about."

"What happened to my ship?" Mitchell repeated.

Steve rolled his eyes. "I cannot believe this. How can I best express this to you?" He rubbed his hands together and raised his voice slightly. "You're at the actual end of a universe right now. In a little bit, as you measure time, there won't be anything left of this universe. Do you understand that? Does your tiny little brain get that you're not the most important thing in this universe right now?"

Mitchell clenched his fists so hard his nails started to dig into his palms. "What. The. Hell. Happened. To. My. Ship?"

Steve threw his hands up in exasperation. "I give up. I give up. Your stupid little ship is *fine*. Your crew is *fine*." He waved a dismissive hand. "Or as fine as they can be considering you have them zipping around the galaxy in a rusty tin can that's practically falling apart at the seams. Everybody's *fine*. Are you happy now? Do you feel like you have a grasp on reality once again? Now that you can breathe a sigh of relief about all your silly little idiot subordinates back home do you think you can stop and take one godforsaken moment and recognize that *the entirety of the multiverse does not revolve around you?!*"

Mitchell exhaled slowly and let his hands relax. He felt a weight drift from his shoulders. His ship was okay.

He watched as Steve fumed, fidgety with frustration and agitation. A small smile tugged at the corners of his mouth. "Was it something I said?"

Steve jabbed a finger at Mitchell and grumbled something unintelligible. He took a step back and held up a hand as he composed himself.

"You know," Steve said after a few seconds. "I shouldn't have to say this, but I'm not exactly the kind of being you want to antagonize."

"Of course not," Mitchell replied evenly. "You're the kind of being who thinks the multiverse revolves around *him*."

Steve smiled and spread out his arms. "But, of course. Because it does. And just like that, you've learned your first valuable lesson of the multiverse."

"What kind of game are you playing at?"

Steve didn't say anything for a second. He shook his head in disbelief. "Game? *Game*?" He looked around at the asteroid that was slowly falling apart around them with an exaggerated gesture. "What part of any of this strikes you as a *game*, Captain? As a source of *childish amusement*?" He jabbed a finger at Mitchell. "What kind of idiot fool do you take me for? I didn't bring you to the *end of a universe* for a game, Gavin Mitchell. And the fact that you think so suggests that *you're still not getting it*."

"I don't have time for this."

"Excuse me?"

With an effort, Mitchell pushed past Steve, moving in the direction he had seen Savina heading in.

"We're not done here," Steve said after him.

"I am."

Suddenly Steve was standing in front of him again. "Where the hell do you think you're going?"

"To help." Mitchell placed a hand on Steve's shoulder and pointedly pushed him out of the way.

Steve gaped at the spot where Mitchell had touched him and then he was in front of the captain again. He wordlessly gesticulated with his hands for a few seconds, clearly at a loss for words.

Mitchell folded his arms. "I don't know what this is, but I'm certainly glad I have the opportunity to see it. Because you look like a real idiot when you don't know what to say."

Steve glared at him and dropped his hands. "What exactly do you think you're going to help with?" he asked. "Last time I checked, you don't have any experience with saving the universe."

"That's the Unity out there," Mitchell said.

"Oh, I'm very much aware of what's out there," Steve said. "And here's a fun fact that you clearly haven't taken to heart yet: That's *all* that's out there. There aren't any other surviving oasis's out in the Abyss. Hell, it's rather remarkable that this one's survived for as long as it has. So there's nothing out there for you to save these people for. Don't you get it? The Unity is the top of the food chain in this dimension and what's about to happen here is simply the natural order of things."

"*Natural?*" Mitchell barked at him. "This is far from natural. This is an invading force hellbent on exterminating entire species in its path."

Steve nodded. "Yes. And another way of describing that is 'nature.'"

"You're out of your damn mind," Mitchell said.

"On that, I agree with you," Steve replied. "I'm

starting to wonder what the hell I was thinking, bringing you here in the first place. I knew you were slow on the update, Gavin, but I can't possibly dumb it down for you anymore here."

"What did you bring me here for?" Mitchell asked.

"Why do you think?"

"I don't know."

Steve frowned. "Then maybe you're not thinking about it very hard."

Mitchell chewed the inside of his cheek. "I think you're losing touch."

Steve raised his eyebrows. "Losing touch with what?"

"Your humanity."

Steve rolled his eyes again. "Oh, my goodness. You really don't listen to a damn thing I say, do you? My *humanity*?" He made a show of gagging.

Mitchell waved dismissively with his hand. "Call it whatever you want. Your humanity. Your conscience. Your *soul*."

"I should warn you that if you try to hug me, I will literally snap you out of existence and I won't feel the slightest bit guilty about it."

"Exactly," Mitchell said. "That's why I'm here."

Steve shook his head. "I cannot believe how far off base you are right now. No, I mean, I *can*. But, I *can't*. Do you understand? What am I saying? Of course you don't."

Mitchell took a step back and pointed at the small handful of people in the promenade. "You can help them."

Steve blinked and shook his head. "I'm sorry now?"

"You can help these people. That's why you brought me here. To remind you," Mitchell said. "They don't have to die."

"As a matter of fact, yes they do," Steve replied. "It's the end of the universe around here. Once their entire universe is gone, they don't have much of a point for existing anymore."

"You brought me here. You can bring them someplace else."

Steve gaped at him. "Someplace *else*? Are you even listening to yourself? More importantly, are you even listening to *me*? There is no place else, Mitchell. Do you realize how close we are to your dimension? Cosmically speaking, we're basically two floors down. I bring them up two floors, assuming they survive the trip, all I've done is moved them to a higher section of a building that's *burning down*."

"Then why don't you put out the damn fire," Mitchell snapped.

"Put out the..." Steve shook his head. "I'm sorry, I think we've gotten mixed up in our metaphors here. You realize when I say 'fire' I mean The Unity, yes?"

"You're clearly more powerful than anyone else around here," Mitchell said.

"Look, I don't mind a little bit of flattery, but read the room, Gavin, I don't really think it's going to help your case."

"If you're so damn powerful, why don't you just wipe out the Unity yourself?" It was a question that came across like a threat. "Maybe you can't."

"Or maybe it's because you really don't want me going around snapping my fingers and deciding which races and cultures just get wiped out," Steve replied. "Who's to say that once I'm done with the Unity, I don't come after your precious United Planetary Alliance? There's a pointless thought exercise for you."

"The UPA is nothing like the Unity."

Steve rolled his eyes in an over exaggerated fashion. "Oh *please*, Captain. Do you know where culture goes to die? The UPA. Over one hundred and thirty distinct and unique species are a part of your illustrious alliance, although you'd never know it."

"What the hell are you talking about?"

"Your Alliance homogenizes its every member. All the rough edges are aggressively smoothed over. After all, that's why the Oxean have been rejected no less than a dozen times from joining."

"The Oxean Syndicate-"

"Is no less valid than say, the Haka," Steve said. "Just because they believe in aggressively culling the weaker members of their species and the Haka believe in aggressive overpopulation. And, as I recall, didn't the Haka practice ritual cannibalism before being accepted into your precious little Planetary Alliance? The UPA doesn't promote unity through cooperation and understanding. It promotes unity through making everyone boring and by cutting everybody down to the same size."

Mitchell shook his head and pointed violently at the ground beneath their feet. "These people-"

"Are *dead*. They were dead long before I ever brought you here. That's what you don't seem to understand. That's what they don't understand: They're dead and don't realize it. Or worse, they do realize it and they refuse to accept it," Steve said. "Forget about the generators failing or decades old technology unable to hold out indefinitely. It's basic *math*. There are only so many equation variations for their stupid little computers to cycle through for the quantum sound shield. The numbers are large, but the math is ridiculously *simple*. Eventually it's going to come up zero." He shrugged. "And they know it. They tried their best not to know, they randomized the programs so it wouldn't be so obvious. But the clock has been ticking down since the moment they turned on that quantum sound shield." He smiled widely. "And guess what today is?"

Mitchell stared at him. "You're a monster."

"Oh, come on," Steve pouted. "Now you're just being mean. I didn't do this. They did it to themselves."

"You can still save them."

Steve shook his head. "How are we back to this? I swear, I don't know why I even bother."

Mitchell shoved past him.

"What the hell do you think you're doing?" Steve asked.

"Whatever I can," Mitchell shot back over his shoulder.

"Which is nothing," Steve said. "It is literally *nothing*. There is nothing you can do."

"At least it's something."

Steve shook his head. "No, actually it's not. That's what nothing is. The absence of something."

Mitchell didn't respond.

"Fine." Steve sighed. "I'll dumb it down for you even more."

Steve snapped his fingers, and everything went white.

34

MITCHELL VOMITED and dropped to his knees.

The contents of his stomach sprayed out across an expanse of whiteness.

He propped his hands against his thighs for support as everything spun around him. His stomach churned again, threatening to expel what was left. He took a couple of steady, shallow breaths and the nausea faded.

But the whiteness around him did not.

Mitchell slowly got back to his feet. His equilibrium was off, and everything felt unbalanced. Except, that wasn't it.

Mitchell turned in a slow circle, his mind trying to process what he was seeing and failing.

Everything around him, above him and below him was just white.

No structures.

No people.

Nothing.

Except white.

The only way Mitchell knew that he had even finished

his circle was that he was suddenly facing Steve, who hadn't been there a second ago.

"Where the hell am I now?" Mitchell croaked. He coughed and felt his stomach threaten to rebel again.

"You're nowhere." Steve's black suit was a sharp contrast against the overwhelming whiteness of everything.

"Where the hell is that?" Mitchell asked, his voice sounding a little more normal.

"No place you know," Steve replied evenly. "Let's be honest, I could go through the trouble of explaining all the science behind your current location, but you wouldn't understand it and it's really not your fault. You simply *can't* understand it." He tapped the side of his head. "Your brain is too underdeveloped. This isn't a reflection on you, so much as it is for your entire species. There's an entire division of cosmic math that the human race wouldn't be able to understand for at least, I don't know, a hundred thousand years. Maybe more. Probably more. Definitely more. Assuming, of course, you even get that far. Based on my calculations? The Unity won't even give you an extra one hundred years." He held a hand to his mouth in mock embarrassment. "Oops, spoilers."

Mitchell glared at him and turned around again, looking for something other than the white. "Send me back."

"Send you back? Back where?"

Mitchell shot him a look over his shoulder. "Back to those people."

Steve stared at him for a second. "You can't be serious."

Mitchell started walking. He wasn't sure where he was heading or if he was heading anywhere. But he had to move. If he just stood still, the white seemed to close in on him.

"They're already dead, Mitchell," Steve said. "There's nothing to go back to. Unless you're eager to get on with the end of your own existence."

Mitchell stumbled to a stop. He felt like he had just done six shots of M'reth ale. "What's wrong with me?"

"Like I said before, it's not easy to move between the membranes of the multiverse unprotected." Steve stepped up alongside him. His footsteps made a sharp clipping sound against the white. "I suppose I could have taken the time to properly prepare you, but you don't really make it easy for that."

Mitchell lifted his head slightly and looked at him out of the corner of his eye. "What's your point?"

"Among other things, you need to learn a little patience," Steve said. "Not only would it make my life a little easier, but it would make yours infinitely easier."

"You're a bastard," Mitchell said, rubbing the heel of his hand into his eye.

"A bastard? Please." Steve made a dismissive sound under his breath. "If I was a bastard, I wouldn't bother with you people. If I was a bastard, I would just go home to my little slice of paradise and watch as the Unity consumes you all."

"You let those people die," Mitchell said. "You let an entire universe die."

Steve sighed and shook his head. "How do you not understand this? They were already dead. There was no way for them not to be dead. I have a great many abilities, but none of them include the ability to *raise the dead*."

"Except they weren't dead," Mitchell said. He felt himself slowly getting better. The nausea had passed. His limbs still felt a little wobbly and the disorientation of the white around him threatened to overwhelm him at any given moment. But otherwise, he was feeling more like himself. "They were *alive*. They were *fighting*. After their entire universe fell, they were still *fighting*."

Something flared behind Steve's eyes. "Yes. *Exactly*. And what were they fighting for? There was no scenario in which they were going to win. It was the very definition of an exercise in futility."

"Maybe they were holding on to faith," Mitchell said.

"*Faith?*" Steve laughed. "Faith in what?"

"Faith that a higher power would come to their rescue."

Steve stopped laughing and pointed to himself. "You mean me, of course. Once again, I'm flattered. But you still don't get it. I keep trying to show you the bigger picture and you don't get it." He took a deep breath. "Everybody's going to *die*. The Unity won't stop. It can't be stopped. There is no last minute solution that's going to save everything. The Unity will finish with one reality and then move on to the next. They'll just keep going and going and going. Until there's nothing left. It is *inevitable*. All that's left is for you to make your peace with it."

Mitchell didn't speak. For some reason, Steve's words seemed to echo in the white around them.

He studied Steve's face, watching his eyes, and then finally recognized something there: desperation.

"Peace," Mitchell whispered.

Steve's words finally clicked.

"That's what all this has been about," he said.

Steve shook his finger at Mitchell. "Don't you tease me."

"You want us to give up."

"'Give up' sounds like such a downer," Steve said. "I just want you to accept your reality. I want you to go to your death with a little dignity. There's no dignity in fighting against an abyss that you will never beat."

"The hell there isn't."

"Trust me, Mitchell. I've seen it played out countless times already. The people of Apaka refused to accept their reality. They railed against the darkness and what did it get them? An extra fifty years?"

"It's better than nothing."

"And what about the children born into that," Steve said. "They were born to die."

"We all die," Mitchell said. "It's the nature of life."

"They were born to die with no future. There was nothing for them to contribute. There was *nothing* for them to experience, save for the dread of knowing that one day, their collective number was going to come up and the Unity would take them all."

"You're insane."

Steve shrugged. "To you, perhaps. But do you care what the family pet thinks of you as you have it neutered?"

"Dignity in death," Mitchell said with a scowl.

"Dignity in death," Steve repeated a smile. "You have nothing else. The Unity will take anything and everything. It takes your *soul*. You realize that? Your very soul. What makes you *you*. And the Unity will take it." He shrugged. "What's left except for your dignity?"

Mitchell turned away from him. "Send me back to my ship."

Steve shook his head. "That's it? I go through all this trouble to bring you enlightenment and all you have to say is 'Send me back to my ship'?"

"This isn't enlightenment," Mitchell said. "It's cosmic euthanasia."

"You say that like it's a bad thing. Have you seen the state of cosmos around here? I'm not suggesting you take up collective suicide, but I certainly wouldn't begrudge anyone for wanting to check out before the Unity checked in."

"Send me back to my ship," Mitchell repeated.

"Not even a thank you? I do believe I'm a little offended," Steve said. "Tell me, what are you going to do when you get back? Don't go starting any religions in my name. That never ends well for me."

"I'm not going to tell anybody about you," Mitchell said. "Other than you're a pain in the ass. If the whole point of all this was to convince me that my entire universe needs to just lay down and die quietly. Well, you wasted both our time."

Steve frowned. "That's…disappointing."

"Now you know how I feel when you didn't save those people," Mitchell said. He folded his arms. "Are we finished here?"

Steve stared at him for a moment, his lips curled into a disapproving sneer. "I guess we are."

And then he snapped his fingers.

35

USS DEFIANCE

THE OVERHEAD LIGHTS FLICKERED, and Sadler stirred as she was roused from Sharon's spell. She felt disoriented; her head fuzzy as though she had just spent hours in front of a screen. She rubbed her brow. "That's..."

"*Bullshit*," Rabkin said. His voice sounded extra raspy and he coughed, clearing out his throat.

"Excuse me?" Sharon said, looking mildly perturbed.

Rabkin got to his feet. "It's just another damn campfire story. Because if it wasn't, you people would be the biggest idiots in all of creation since the Democratic Socialist Party of the Twenty-First Century."

Sharon frowned. "While I don't disagree that we made some questionable decisions-"

"*Questionable?*" Rabkin cut her off. "Questionable?"

Sadler moved around the desk, positioning herself between the two of them. "Alright, doc, let's just take a minute here. I think we're still missing a handful of relevant details."

Rabkin waved her off. "If even *half* of what this green

haired witch just said was true, we're in this mess because of them."

"It wouldn't be the first time we've been caught up in a problem of another race's making," Sadler said in an attempt to be diplomatic. But it sounded hollow even to her.

"This is not the fault of my people," Sharon said. "We warned Gary-"

"I don't give a damn about Gary," Rabkin said. "He sounds like an idiot asshole, too. But he wasn't the idiot who kept sending waves of his peers down to get *slaughtered*."

Sharon's hands balled into fists and her face tightened. "I would advise you to watch your tone, little man. I am here to help you, but my goodwill does not extend to allowing you to judge me."

"Good thing I don't need your permission to judge you then," Rabkin said.

"You would be foolish to do so."

Rabkin waved his hand at her. "Well, it sounds like you people wrote the book on doing foolish things, so I'll take your word for it."

Something sparked in Sharon's eyes. An electrical glow. Sadler immediately recalled what happened the last time Sharon used a portion of her abilities.

Rabkin jammed a finger at Sharon. "You people damned all of existence because God forbid anyone other than you should step foot in your little paradise."

Sadler held up both of her hands and leveled her gaze at Rabkin. "Okay, that's *enough*."

Rabkin's eyes moved from Sharon to Sadler, but she didn't budge. He grunted something under his breath and took a step back.

Sharon glowered at them. "We made the ultimate sacrifice for all of you and had we not, this conversation would not be taking place right now. If the Abyss had gained access to our home dimension, they would have been able to create a feeding loop that would have consumed from both ends of the Stack." She snapped her fingers. "And everything would have been over like *that*. Again, I believe the words you are looking for are, 'Thank you.'"

Sadler turned to Sharon. "You're not helping matters either. Maybe you're some all-powerful entity from a higher dimension, but until Captain Mitchell gets back here, I'm in charge and I don't really care for your attitude either."

Sharon looked at Sadler and tilted her head. "You are not what I expected."

"I'm going to choose to take that as a compliment," Sadler said.

Sharon shrugged. "Do with it as you will. My words seem to fall on deaf ears around here."

Sadler took a deep breath in order to avoid snapping at the entity standing in front of her who could probably break their ship in two with her pinky.

"Not so easy, is it?" Rabkin asked.

Sadler glared at him out of the corner of her eye. "Now I know why the captain's always in such a mood when you're hanging around on the bridge." She turned back to Sharon. "Speaking of our captain, you said you know where he is?"

Sharon nodded. "Yes. I believe Steve has taken him to another dimension."

"What the hell is that supposed to mean?" Rabkin asked.

She looked at him coolly. "I believe it's fairly self-explanatory."

"Okay, you know, I'd like to get through five minutes here without the two of you throwing jabs at each other like we're in a freshman's debate challenge," Sadler snapped. "So here's what we're going to do. I'm going to ask questions." She pointed at Sharon. "*You're* going to answer them." She turned to Rabkin. "And *you're* going to shut the hell up. Everybody understand?"

Both of Rabkin's bushy eyebrows went up. "Am I actually supposed to answer that? Because it feels like a trap."

Sadler shook her head and turned back to Sharon. "Can you take us to Captain Mitchell?"

"Yes. But it's not going to be an easy journey."

"Of course it isn't," Sadler muttered, rubbing her forehead. "Why the hell should anything be easy around here?"

As if in response to her the ship shuddered around them. Lights flickered, threatening to go out completely before settling on just dimming slightly.

Sadler opened a channel to engineering. "Mr. Warrick?"

"Is this important? Because I don't really have time to chitchat right now," Warrick barked in response. "Whatever the hell that green haired broad up there was doing to Keane also did a number on our structural integrity, which in turn is putting even more strain on the power relays. So I'm kind of in the middle of literally holding the ship together with my bare hands!"

"In addition, I find it highly unlikely that your ship would survive the trip between dimensions," Sharon said. "Given its current difficulty simply surviving in space."

"Is that the green haired witch that nearly blew out half of deck five with her damn cosmic hoodoo?" Warrick shouted. "You tell her-"

Sadler gritted her teeth. "Never mind." She quickly

closed the channel and looked at Rabkin. "I think we're all going to die out here."

"Why the hell do you think I've been trying to get off this ship?" Rabkin muttered. "It's a damn coffin dressed up as a starship."

"Why do you insist on traveling through the void of space in such a derelict heap?" Sharon asked.

"I ask myself the same question every damn day," Rabkin said. "I haven't come up with a good answer yet." He looked at Sadler. "You?"

She rubbed her face tiredly. "I'm just trying to put as much distance between me and my parents."

The ship shuddered violently again. Sadler and Rabkin nearly lost their footing, grabbing the desk to avoid falling to the ground altogether. Sharon didn't so much as twitch.

Sparks exploded from the consoles around them and an alarm started blaring.

"Dammit!" Sadler exclaimed, opening the channel to engineering again. "Warrick, what the hell is going on?"

But there was no response and a second later the ship abruptly pitched forward. Rabkin and Sadler lost their grip on the desk, tumbling to the floor.

Then the lights went out.

36

KEANE AND ZEMBLE found the officer assigned to Calloway's quarters on the floor of the corridor unconscious.

"He wasn't like this when I left him here earlier," Zemble said.

Keane knelt down to check for a pulse as Zemble entered Calloway's quarters. "He's still alive. What have you got in there?"

"No Calloway," Zemble replied from inside.

"Shit." Keane got back to his feet. "What the hell happened?"

Zemble stepped back out into the corridor. "I'm assuming that's a rhetorical question, considering we both know that I don't possess any ability to perceive other people's point of views."

Keane pulled out his communicator. "Keane to Calloway?"

"I don't think it's likely she's going to answer," Zemble said.

"You also thought it was a good idea to leave her in her quarters."

Zemble pointed to the unconscious officer. "It's not like I left her unsupervised. But also," he held up Calloway's communicator. "I don't think she's going to answer because she left this behind."

"Nobody likes a smartass," Keane said, opening a channel to sickbay.

"Present company excluded, of course," Zemble said.

"This is Commander Keane. I need a medical response on deck six. I've got an officer down with a possible concussion." Once he got a confirmation he disconnected and pocketed his communicator. He stepped past Zemble to examine Calloway's quarters.

Nothing seemed to be out of order. The sheets on her bed were in a mess, but there was nothing that indicated there had been any kind of struggle.

"You see something I don't?" Zemble asked from the doorway.

Keane looked over his shoulder at him. "What's with the attitude?"

"Attitude?" Zemble asked innocently.

Keane gave him a look.

Zemble shrugged. "I don't like being kept in the dark about potential threats on the ship."

"She wasn't a threat." Keane stepped back out into the corridor.

"By what metrics did you determine that?" Zemble asked.

"What the hell kind of question is that?"

"If she's infected with the Unity-"

"We don't know that she is," Keane said, cutting him off.

Zemble just grunted.

Keane tugged at his collar again. "At the time we didn't know that she was. All we knew was that she communicated with the Unity on Carlock. None of Rabkin's scans turned up anything out of the ordinary on her. So my orders were to basically keep her under close observation."

"By enlisting her into a security detail?"

"Keep your friends close and potential enemies closer."

"I don't believe that's how it goes," Zemble said. "I'm concerned because you didn't share those orders with me."

"*Share?*" Keane repeated.

"I'm fairly certain you're familiar with the concept."

"Something happen during your jaunt into another dimension that made you forget how the chain of command works around here?"

Zemble pointed to Keane. "Head of security." He pointed to himself. "Next in command of security. Did I get it right?"

"It was on a need-to-know basis," Keane said. bristling slightly.

"As your number two around here I would think I would need to know."

Keane held his hands out, palms up. "Disappointment is a way of life out here."

"I don't like it."

"Oh well," Keane said unhelpfully.

"Calloway's not our enemy," Zemble said.

Keane wordlessly pointed to the unconscious officer.

Zemble just grunted again.

Keane sighed. "Look, I like Erin, too."

"Don't think I'm not worried about that, too," Zemble said. "You like too many of the female officers on this ship. It's not big enough for you to like so many women."

Keane glared at him and continued, through gritted

teeth, "What I'm trying to say is I don't think Erin's aware of what she may or may not be."

Zemble took a second to absorb that. "You think she's some kind of sleeper agent?"

"Maybe." Keane shrugged. "Maybe not. I don't know. What I do know is that this doesn't look good. We need to find her before she does anything else that's going to look worse."

The ship shuddered around them and Keane held out a hand, bracing himself against the corridor wall. They stared up at the flickering lights, watching as they threatened to go out completely before just dimming slightly.

"What the hell was that?" Keane asked.

"It's a day ending in 'y' so it must just be the ship falling apart around us," Zemble said.

"I don't like how you say that so calmly."

"I've made my peace with my creator," Zemble said. "I'm not necessarily looking forward to death, but it's not something I'm particularly afraid of." He paused and then added, "Is this a bad time to talk to you about accepting Jesus into your heart?"

Keane flexed his newly restored left am. "I think I'm doing pretty good without Jesus right now. But thanks for asking."

"Maybe you're doing so well because God wants you to have every opportunity to turn yourself over to him," Zemble said.

"Seriously?"

"You did just suffer a near-death experience. Is there a better time to have this discussion?"

"I thought you were pissed off at me?"

"Not so much that I'd want you to rot in Hell for all of eternity," Zemble replied.

Keane opened his mouth and then closed it. He

snapped his fingers. "Wait a minute, where did you say you found Erin before?"

"Cargo bay Two."

Keane rubbed his chin. "Shit."

"What?"

"I think I know where she is." Keane started for the lift.

"Why would she go back to Cargo Bay Two?" Zemble asked, following him.

Keane didn't answer.

"What else don't I know?" Zemble growled.

Before Keane could say anything, the ship shuddered violently again. Zemble's quick reflexes kept Keane from hitting the floor of the corridor face first.

The consoles in Calloway's quarters exploded into sparks and an alarm started blaring down the length of the corridor.

The ship abruptly pitched forward and then everything went dark.

37

AFTER A FEW SECONDS of darkness a dim light flickered on, casting Rabkin's office in a hazy red glow.

Sadler grabbed the desk and pulled herself back up. There was a loud groan behind her as Rabkin did the same.

Sharon stood in the same spot, unmoving.

Sadler's stance felt unsteady. There was no real direction in space, yet she could distinctly feel the ship tilted in the *wrong* direction. Sadler took an experimental step away from the desk and nearly tripped, as though she had forgotten she wasn't carrying an extra thirty pounds. She patted her torso. Nothing seemed to be missing. But her weight definitely felt off. That meant something was wrong with the gravity plating.

"I'm gonna feel that in the morning," Rabkin said, pulling himself into his seat. "Assuming there is a morning at this point and honestly, I think I'd be okay if there wasn't."

The alarm had faded away, but all the consoles in Rabkin's office were blank and judging by the sounds of the confused nurses in the rest of sickbay, Sadler figured things weren't any better out there either.

Sadler looked at Sharon, but she didn't say anything. The green haired woman just stood in the same spot where she had been standing before, apparently completely unfazed by whatever was happening.

Sadler started to say something, but then thought better of it. Instead she opened a channel to engineering. "Warrick?"

There was a brief moment of static and then the chief engineer's voice came through, slightly garbled. "And what the hell do you want me to do about it, Westin? Hold the damn cables with my bare hands so you can watch me get fried like a Draeddur turkey?"

"Mr. Warrick," Sadler said again, attempting to draw his attention to the open channel.

"Yeah, yeah, I hear you," Warrick said.

Sadler paused. "Are you talking to me now?"

"Well, I'm sure as hell not going to waste any more of my breath talking to Westin," Warrick replied, his voice almost disappearing in a burst of static.

"Warrick," Sadler said, her voice straining with her lack of patience. "What the hell happened?"

"What the hell do you think happened?"

"I'm not in the mood to play twenty questions."

Warrick started to say something else, but it was lost in the static. After it cleared again, Sadler heard him say, "We just lost main power. Auxiliary power is holding, but we've got two hull breaches on decks eleven and nine. I'm diverting power from the gravity plating to keep us all from getting sucked out into space. What the hell is that green haired devil lady doing to my ship now?"

Sadler looked at Sharon expectantly.

Sharon held out her hand, palms open. "I am not

doing anything, except being patient and I would not think that my patience is going to threaten to destroy your derelict space vessel. But I have been wrong once or twice before."

"Other than being a pain in the ass, I don't think she's doing anything, Warrick," Sadler said.

"Well someone is doing something on my ship they're not supposed to be doing," Warrick said. There was a burst of static that drowned out the next few words. When it cleared up, Sadler heard, "-massive particle energy spikes. It's putting a strain on our structural integrity, which, in case you've forgotten, is already under too much of a strain as it is."

Sadler looked at Sharon again, who shook her head. "It is still not me"

"Of course it's not," Sadler muttered. "Okay, Warrick, how long before we get main power back up?"

"If whatever's generating these particle spikes doesn't stop? Never."

The ship shuddered again.

"I don't like the sound of never, Warrick," Sadler said.

"What do you want from me? I can't just change the nature of the English language," Warrick said.

"Warrick…"

"Look, maybe if my ship wasn't already in dire need of repair, I could give you a better timetable," Warrick said. "But she's not and we don't have the time to make the kind of repairs needed to keep us all from *dying*."

"This is why I wanted to retire," Rabkin said.

"Auxiliary power won't hold for much longer," Warrick said. "Especially not under these kinds of conditions. All it's going to take is one stutter along the backup power grid and the forcefields containing those hull breaches are going to blink out and half the ship is going to follow. And in case you're feeling optimistic about those odds for some reason, the other half of the ship is going to watch in horror as it breaks apart around them. Our best bet is to find out what the hell is causing those particle wave spikes and get it to stop."

Sadler took a deep breath. "Okay. So what's causing the particle wave spikes?"

38

CALLOWAY STARED down at the device before her, not entirely certain what she had done.

She understood what the numbers on the small screen were. One set of numbers counting down. Another counting up. Dimly, she knew what was going to happen when the numbers reached their end points.

But Calloway couldn't wrap her head around the concept that *she* had done *this*, whatever this was.

Around her Cargo Bay Two was awash in dim red light, creating long intimidating shadows that encircled her like a barrier. The alarm hadn't even startled her when it started and when it shut off, she barely even noticed it.

Calloway was completely and utterly focused on the device.

She tried to remember how, specifically, she had arrived here, but again her memories were a blurry haze. But she still *knew*. In her bones, in her heart, she *knew* the truth.

She looked down at her hands, staring at them as if they belonged to somebody else. A notion that would have been crazy to even contemplate any other day. But today? Now? These weren't her hands anymore. No. They belonged to the voice in her head that wasn't hers.

She looked past her hands at the device again. Around her she could hear the ship groaning as the numbers raced towards their conclusions.

Calloway took a shuddering breath and slowly got to her feet. She needed to get out of there, but she couldn't convince the rest of her to leave. The voice in her head that didn't belong to her had taken over most of her body. Now she was just riding shotgun.

"Calloway?"

At first she thought it was in her head. The Voice perhaps? But it didn't sound like the Voice. The Voice didn't sound like anything, really. Well, nothing and everything. It was both alien and familiar. It was driving her crazy.

"Erin? Are you in here?"

Calloway closed her eyes in sweet relief, tears trickling down her cheeks. It wasn't in her head. There was somebody here looking for her and it was *Zemble*.

She opened her mouth, wanting to call out his name, wanting to shout at the top of her lungs, but nothing came out. Because, of course, the Voice was in charge now.

The device in front of her made a new noise, an alarming sound and Calloway felt the ship strain around her.

Her eyes shot open and she looked down to find the numbers on the device speeding up.

"Erin?" Zemble's voice was much closer now, right over her shoulder.

Calloway turned around to find not just Zemble standing there, but Keane as well.

She was relieved and then confused.

Something about her surprised them. Scared them? She couldn't tell. Their reactions…

Keane tensed up. Zemble's face was a mask that she couldn't read, but she knew that something wasn't right.

Did they know what was wrong with her? Of course not. After all, the Voice was in *her head*. They couldn't see something that was in her head.

But what explanation would there be for what she was doing here?

And then she noticed the fusion pistol in Keane's hand.

Keane's eyes focused on hers. If she had been in control of her body, she would have looked away, uncomfortable. But the Voice didn't have her insecurities.

"Calloway," Keane said slowly. "*Erin*, you need to step away from that right now."

Of course.

Calloway didn't move. She *wanted* to move. She kept shouting at her limbs to listen to her. Screaming at them. But she didn't move.

Keane flexed his grip around the fusion pistol. He tried to look past her at the device and the Voice shifted her body to block his view. She could read the anxiety, the fear in his eyes. What had she done?

"Erin," Keane said, clearly trying to keep his voice steady. Something in her face, in her eyes, bothered him. He struggled to keep his gaze locked on her. "I'm not going to ask again."

She understood the implied threat and so did the Voice. It didn't matter what Keane was or wasn't going to do, because the Voice wasn't going to give him the opportunity either way.

What happened next took less than ten seconds.

Keane's finger tightened around the trigger of the fusion pistol.

Calloway felt her body move, covering the distance between them in a single step. Everything was a blur of speed around her.

Her hands came into contact with Keane and then he was flying through the air, crashing into the cargo containers on the opposite side of the cargo bay.

What the hell was *that*? How had she done *that*? That wasn't possible. That defied the laws of gravity. The laws of physics. And yet...

The Voice moved Calloway's body, turning on Zemble. She wanted to warn him. Tell him to run. She could feel her mouth open, but nothing came out.

Zemble didn't move. He didn't make any threatening gestures. He didn't even look to see if Keane was okay. His focus was entirely on Calloway.

Behind her the device made another sound and she knew that it was almost done. Everything was almost done and soon none of this would matter to her anymore.

Zemble brought his hands up slowly. "Erin, I'm not here to hurt you," he spoke in a surprisingly soft tone of voice.

She wanted to tell him that he should be. She wanted to tell him that the Voice was going to hurt him just as it had hurt Keane. She wanted to tell him not to waste his time trying to talk to her, because she wasn't in charge anymore. But, of course, she couldn't say any of this. She simply watched helplessly, wondering what her body was going to do next.

Zemble looked like he was going to take a step forward. But when Calloway's hands turned to fists, he stopped.

"Okay," he said. "It's okay."

Calloway wanted to laugh. This was so far removed from 'okay' they might as well be in a different galaxy.

"This isn't you," Zemble said. "I know it's not you. I also know that you're still in there."

Sure, she was still in here, but what did that matter? She wasn't the one driving anymore.

Zemble paused, like he was waiting for a response. But the Voice wasn't interested in having a conversation with him.

"Whatever's going on, we can help you," Zemble continued. "*I* can help you."

There was a noise at the back of her throat. What was it? A laugh? A sob? Was it her or the Voice?

Something on Zemble's face changed. Had he heard the noise she made?

"You're not in control of your actions," Zemble said. "This isn't your fault. I understand that. There's something inside of you that doesn't belong. But it's not who you are."

He had no idea who she was. *What* she was. Hell, neither did she for that matter.

"Whatever's happening to you right now, you're still you," Zemble said. "Do you understand me? You're still Erin Calloway."

Was she? She wasn't so sure about that anymore. The Voice felt like so much more than her.

"You're still you," he repeated.

No, she wasn't. And worse, she wasn't certain that she had ever really been herself in the first place.

New alarms went off as systems began failing across the ship.

"You know how I know this?" Zemble asked. "Because you haven't tried to stop me yet. There's still a part of you in there that's *you*. And you, Erin Calloway, don't want to hurt anybody."

Sure, she thought, *that's why I tossed Keane across the cargo bay like a rag doll.*

Zemble nodded as if she had said something out loud. Had she? She didn't think she had. Her ears felt stuffy and Zemble's words sounded like they were coming from across a distance. But surely she would have heard herself speak, wouldn't she?

Zemble took a slow, steadying breath. "I wasn't entirely honest about what happened when Steve sent me away. I remember everything that happened. From your perspective, I was only gone minutes. But from mine, I was gone for *years*. And they were terrible years. I experience horrific things. The people there they were…" he trailed off for a moment, lost in a painful memory. His eye snapped back in focus on Calloway. "They were monsters. And I know what that sounds like coming from someone who looks like me. But these people, these creatures, they didn't have any framework or understanding of love, kindness, compassion. Cruelty was written in their DNA the same way that ours says that we need to breathe air." He paused again. "I think I might have been in Hell. At least that's what I thought when I was there. Now…" He shook his head and shrugged. "I don't know what it was.

"Every day I was there, they tried to break me. Physically, emotionally, spiritually. They tried to convince me that this world had never existed. That I was crazy. That I was mad. And you know what? They almost did it. Every single day. They almost broke me. Every day. *Almost*.

"My faith was what saved me every day," Zemble said. "My faith in a God who I knew wouldn't abandon me, that wouldn't forsake me. A God who, no matter what, had my back. I didn't know if I was going to make it back here. But I knew that even if I didn't, I wasn't alone there."

Zemble took a cautious step towards her.

"And you're not alone here, Erin," he said. "This thing that's in you, it doesn't have to control you. I know that it feels like it does, but it doesn't. Not really. Nobody's abandoned you. We haven't and God certainly hasn't. You just need to have a little faith, Erin. It doesn't take much." He held up one hand, his finger and thumb so close together they were nearly touching. "No more than a mustard seed's worth. Do you hear me? Maybe you don't believe that we can help you and you don't have to. Just believe that God can."

Something in Zemble's voice, his words, they struck her in an unexpected way.

The Voice struck back.

She could feel the Voice pushing her, manipulating her body like a puppet. She watched as her hands came up towards Zemble. She knew what was going to happen and she knew she couldn't stop it.

The Voice was going to have her kill everybody on the ship, including herself and there was nothing she could do about it.

Calloway wanted to scream. She wanted to cry. She wanted everything to *stop*.

Zemble's words rang in her head, fighting for meager scraps with the Voice.

Faith? She wanted to laugh. Faith in *what*?

The Voice dug its claws deeper into her brain.

In the part of her brain that was still hers, Calloway screamed. She felt like maybe the scream escaped her mouth, but she couldn't tell.

Calloway couldn't tell what was real anymore. She couldn't tell what was happening and what she was imagining. She could see Zemble's mouth moving, but it was impossible to separate his voice from the noise in her own head.

Darkness spread across her, enveloping her, threatening to consume her.

Calloway felt a tremble through her body.

Her head jerked back violently as the tremble turned to a seizure. Her body locked up, freezing her in place. Her teeth clamped together painfully. She felt her eyes roll back in her head as everything went dark.

And then...

And then...

And then Erin Calloway was gone.

39

Zemble rushed forward, oblivious to the distortion waves that were coming off the device and caught Calloway as the seizure overtook her. She jerked violently in his arms, black spittle flying from her mouth. And then she stopped, going limp.

Zemble waited a tense second, but there was no other reaction from her.

He checked her pulse. It was steady. He pulled back her eyelid. The blackness that had consumed her eyes was receding and they were returning to their natural state.

There was a grunt from over his shoulder and Keane rushed past to the device. Zemble didn't make any move to help. His focus stayed on Calloway.

Keane's back molars vibrated this close to the device. The distortion waves pulsing off it blurred his vision and unbalanced his equilibrium to the point where he couldn't tell if it was him or the ship that had started pinwheeling.

He grabbed the side of the device with his left hand to steady himself and with his right he moved his fingers across the control panel of the device, punching in what he hoped was the correct command code. In his blurred vision, the graphics of the control panel started to merge together into one swirling psychedelic kaleidoscope.

Keane held his breath as he punched in what he was eighty-five percent sure was the final part of the code and then waited a long tense second.

The device began to power down and he breathed a sigh of relief. His vision cleared and the ache disappeared from his back molars. He staggered back and pulled out his communicator. "Keane to engineering. Good news: we're not going to die today. Your particle wave problem is taken care of."

"Wonderful," Warrick replied sarcastically. "Now all I have to worry about is all the damage around here, including the multiple hull breaches, and hope that I can get main power restored before we all end up decorating the outside of the ship."

"Okay, well, best of luck with that," Keane said.

Warrick grumbled a Vulderran curse and closed the channel.

Keane clicked off the communicator and dropped to the ground, leaning against the closest cargo container.

Nobody spoke for a few minutes.

The red light of the cargo bay dimmed for a little and then brightened.

Keane turned to Zemble. "How is she?"

Zemble shook his head. "I don't know. How are you?"

Keane rubbed his neck and winced. "I feel like I got tossed across a cargo bay."

"Better than getting body parts ripped off?"

"Well, sure," Keane replied. He nodded with his chin at Calloway. "I like how your first reaction was to talk to her after she laid into me."

"Well, it looked painful getting tossed across the cargo

bay," Zemble replied. "Since you had that covered, I figured I'd try something else. Also, I don't like having to hurt my friends."

"Good to have standards," Keane said. "Except that next time, maybe consider the fact that your friend is standing between you and a particle bomb that's going to take out the entire ship."

"Is this really an appropriate time for a performance evaluation?" Zemble asked it.

"I'm afraid that if I don't mention it now, I'll have forgotten about it by the time your annual review comes around," Keane said. He rubbed the side of his face. "What you said to her? About what happened to you. That true?"

Zemble was unable to meet Keane's gaze so he turned back to Calloway, watching as her chest gently rose and fell with each breath. "Yes."

"That's…" Keane trailed off, unsure of what to say.

Zemble understood regardless. "It certainly is."

"Shit," Keane said.

"Yep," Zemble agreed.

"You gonna be okay?"

Zemble looked at him finally. "Are you?"

Keane tugged at his collar again. "Honestly? I have no idea."

Zemble slowly got to his feet, cradling Calloway in his arms. "That sounds about right."

40

"WHAT THE HELL are we doing with a particle bomb on the ship?" Sadler asked as they stepped into the lift.

Sharon looked around at the small space with the detached interest of an archeologist discovering a civilization's primitive form of transportation.

"I'm assuming that's a rhetorical question," Rabkin said.

She shot him a look. "It's not." To the lift, she said, "Bridge."

"You can take it up with Mitchell when he gets back," Rabkin said as the lift starting slowly moving upwards. "Under Directive Fifty-Two, we get up to some sneaky shit."

"So we're carrying around *particle bombs*?"

Rabkin held up a finger. "One. We're carrying *one* particle bomb."

"And what else?"

"How the hell should I know? I'm a doctor, not a weapons inventory specialist."

"Is this really relevant?" Sharon asked.

"Considering we all nearly ended up dead because of it," Sadler said. "Yes, it's very damn relevant."

Sharon frowned. "Your universe is facing extinction."

"I can't help my universe if I'm dead," Sadler snapped.

Sharon was unperturbed. "Then perhaps a better question is: Why do you have a crewman attempting to destroy your ship?"

"That's a hell of a good question." Sadler turned to Rabkin. "You care to field that one?"

Rabkin shook his head. "You've been doing good up until now, I'd rather not step on your toes."

Sadler clasped her hands behind her back. "Ensign Calloway is…"

"Possibly infected by the damn Unity," Rabkin said.

"What happened to not stepping on my toes?"

"You sounded like you were looking for a colorful metaphor," Rabkin replied. "We don't have time for colorful metaphors."

"Since when?"

"Doctor's prerogative."

"I am confused," Sharon interrupted. "You have *another* member of your crew infected by the Unity?"

"It's complicated," Sadler said. "We don't know what-"

"You didn't kill her on the spot?" Sharon asked in disbelief.

"You know, your brother made a similar remark," Rabkin said.

"That's because, despite everything else, my brother is not an idiot."

Rabkin raised his eyebrows in mild surprise. "Consider me fooled."

"I'm not getting in the middle of another thing between you two," Sadler said. "All that matters right now is that Calloway's contained."

Sharon took a deep breath. "I'm beginning to understand my brother's frustration with you. Have you not listened to anything I've said? You don't contain the Unity."

"You did a pretty good job on Keane," Rabkin said.

"That was the exception," Sharon said. "Or perhaps a better descriptor would be: a miracle."

"Miracle?" Rabkin repeated. "You people believe in miracles?"

"Of course we do," Sharon replied. "At the end of the day, there are still things that even my people will be at a loss to explain."

"How 'bout we focus on the things you can explain," Sadler said. "Like how we're going to get the captain."

"Assuming I am able to make the necessary adjustments to your ship and you are willing to accept the possibility of losing a percentage of your crew-"

Sadler turned on her. "Wait, *what*? Why are we losing *anybody*?"

Sharon looked at her coolly. "Because moving between dimensions is not an easy thing for people this far down the Stack to survive. We can make all the necessary preparations. Take all the appropriate precautions, but there is no guarantee that at least one or more of your crew will not make it there or back."

Sadler jabbed her finger at Sharon. "You didn't mention any of this before."

"Obviously I didn't have the opportunity."

"You can't guarantee that somebody will die," Sadler said.

"True," Sharon agreed. "However, I cannot guarantee that everyone will survive the journey either. And honestly, the numbers are not in your favor."

"You can't expect me to sign off on something that's

going to endanger even more lives in an attempt to rescue Captain Mitchell."

"I don't expect you to do anything," Sharon said. "I'm simply providing you with options and telling you what you can expect should you decide to avail yourself of these options."

Sadler turned back to Rabkin and he shook his head.

"I'm extremely biased in this particular situation," he admitted. "Gavin's like a son to me. I would do whatever it took to get him back here."

"Even if it meant sacrificing members of this crew?" Sadler said.

"It's probably a good thing I'm not the captain."

"Bullshit," Sadler said. "You wanted to shove Keane out the damn airlock before she turned him around."

"My point is, it's not a decision that I have to make," Rabkin said.

"Oh, suddenly you don't have an opinion on the matter?" Sadler asked.

"Do you know how old I am? I have an opinion on damn nearly everything," Rabkin shot back.

Sadler nodded. "Okay. So then you're just chickenshit."

"Little lady, need I remind you that not only am I your elder," Rabkin said. "But as the ship's doctor, in many ways I outrank you significantly."

Sadler held out her hands. "By all means, take me off the board. I would love to not have to be the one to decide if it's worth saving our captain and on the plus side, I won't have to listen to you call me 'little lady' anymore."

"You're being remarkably optimistic," Sharon said.

"Excuse me?"

"There's no guarantee that your ship will even survive the modifications long enough to make the trip," Sharon continued. "You could all end up dead before we even leave this dimension."

"I can't decide if I like you or not," Rabkin said.

The lift came to a stop and the doors opened.

Sadler stepped out onto the bridge, feeling an overwhelming dread at having to make an impossible decision. How was she supposed to weigh the lives of the crew against the life of their captain? Captain Mitchell had never hesitated when it came to doing whatever it took to save a member of his crew. But then, he was the captain and she wasn't. This wasn't the kind of thing she had signed up for. One way or another, somebody's blood was going to be on her hands.

Sadler stepped down to the command chair. She was so caught up in her moral dilemma she didn't realize the chair was already occupied. It spun around and she found herself face to face with Captain Gavin Mitchell.

"Oh," she said, startled. "Captain. You're…back?"

"Yeah, I'm back," Mitchell said. He gestured at the red lighting that illuminated the bridge. "Somebody want to tell me what the hell's happened to my ship?"

Sadler blinked and asked, "You want to tell me why we have particle bombs onboard?"

Mitchell looked past her at Rabkin. "What the hell did I miss?"

"Just Commander Sadler really coming into her own as a leader," Rabkin replied. "My balls are rather tender from some quality ball busting."

Sadler dropped her face into her hands. "I don't want to be here anymore." She took a breath and looked up at Mitchell. "I don't have to be here anymore, right? You're back so now I'm not in charge? Please tell me I'm not in charge anymore."

Mitchell opened his mouth, but before he could say anything, Steve spoke up.

"Well, isn't this a pleasant surprise." Steve walked around the command chair with a spring in his step. "It's been a dog's age."

Sharon regarded him with a flat, unamused expression. "This is new for you. Usually, I have to drag you back kicking and screaming."

"That's an exaggeration." Steve turned to Mitchell. "I don't kick. I don't scream. And I am absolutely never dragged anywhere."

"Who the hell is this?" Mitchell asked, nodding at Sharon.

"This," Sadler waved a hand at her, "is Sharon."

"Sharon?" Steve said with a suggestive smirk. "You're still going by that one?"

"It was less work than having to come up with a new one," she replied.

Steve smiled at her. "But that's half the fun."

"Right." Sharon frowned distastefully. "*Fun.*"

"At the very least it's not boring," he said.

"Okay, somebody needs to get me up to speed here," Mitchell said. "And somebody needs to do it quickly because I already used up all my patience in another universe."

"Oh, well, Mitchell, you're in for a treat." Steve walked up to Sharon until they were less than an inch apart. "If you thought one of me was a blast, two is going to blow your mind."

Mitchell turned to Sadler and Rabkin, his eyes desperate for some kind of explanation.

Rabkin grunted. "She says she's Steve's sister."

Which was exactly when Steve bent down and kissed Sharon less like a brother and more like a lover.

41

SADLER BLANCHED at the sight of Steve and Sharon making out. "That's…not exactly how she described their relationship to us."

"Although, I can't say I'm surprised," Rabkin said. "Something about them strikes me as the type of people who focus a little too much on keeping their gene pool clean."

Mitchell cleared his throat loudly.

Steve pulled himself away from Sharon, his hand gently caressing her cheek. "Brother, sister, mother, father. Labels tend to lose their meaning when the total population of your species has dwindled down to just barely double digits."

"To be fair," Sharon said, "the propagation of our people hasn't exactly been on our to-do list."

Steve moved to stand behind Sharon, resting his hands on her shoulders. "True. I'm not entirely sure why, though."

"The last time our species bred was so long ago, none of the survivors even remember it," Sharon said.

"The curse of immortality," Steve said. "Who needs to breed when you can live forever?"

"Except you're not living forever," Rabkin said.

Mitchell looked at him, confused. Rabkin and Sadler quickly brought him up to speed on the secret history of Steve's people and their unfortunate connection to the Unity.

"Sure," Steve said, sounding a little defensive. "Perhaps some of my brethren didn't quite cling to their lives with the same fervent gusto, but I can assure you, I do not share their naked ambivalence. In fact, I very much enjoy being alive. Being alive is *fun*. Whoever said death was the greatest adventure clearly had never thought about what it would be like to dance with a sexy quantum pirate amoeba in a dimension of pure violet sensation." He closed in his eyes in blissful remembrance. "I don't really see any upsides to throwing myself to the Abyss."

"But the pro column for having our entire universe just roll over for the Unity is so long it's absurd, right?" Mitchell said.

The blissful smile dropped from Steve's face. "You're taking my words out of context."

"Dignity in death," Mitchell said. "It's not like there's a lot of wiggle room for interpretation."

"What the hell kind of bullshit is that?" Rabkin said.

Steve stepped away from Sharon. "I don't know how many times I have to explain this to you."

"They do seem disturbingly slow on the uptake," Sharon agreed.

"*You're* all going to *die*," Steve said.

"It's going to happen whether you want it to or not," Sharon said.

"The Unity is going to *win*," Steve picked back up. "This isn't some mindless thought exercise. It's a *fact*."

"No one survives the Unity," Sharon said.

Mitchell looked at Steve coldly. "Except you."

Steve clasped his hands behind his back. "Oh no, my good Captain Mitchell, I am more than aware of the ticking clock of my own mortality. I'm certain that one day there won't be any place left to go that the Unity hasn't already taken." He puffed his chest out. "And I assure you, Captain Mitchell, when my time comes, and it's going to be a long, long, long time before it comes, I won't be cowering in some dark corner, trying to cook up some last minute plan to save myself. But that's a long way off. The Stack is a big place and there's too many dimensions for me to bring the good word to."

"Good word," Rabkin scoffed. "You make it sound like you're a missionary, bringing religious enlightenment to the savages."

Steve's face brightened. "Oh, that's *exactly* what I'm doing."

"You're out of your damn mind," Rabkin said. He waved a hand at Steve and Sharon. "Both of you."

Steve turned to Sharon. "Usually you make a better impression than this."

"It's a frustrating dimension," Sharon said.

"It is," Steve agreed. "I can't decide if I like that or not."

Rabkin smacked his fist against his open palm. "You *idiots*."

"I don't know how many times I have to point this out," Steve said. "But you really shouldn't be antagonizing a being who can literally unravel your DNA with a snap of his fingers."

Rabkin was unfazed. He kept barreling ahead at full speed. "You travel around through the damn multiverse, trying to convince entire universes just to commit suicide because you can't see what's right in front of you."

Steve frowned. "I don't particularly like your tone."

"He has a mood about him," Sharon said.

Rabkin jabbed a finger at them. "This is *your* fault."

"No," Sharon said, drawing the word out slowly as though she was speaking to a small, retarded child. "As I already explained to you, this is *Gary's* fault and he has already paid for his sins with his life."

"But you're the idiots that can't seem to get your act together," Rabkin said. "If the Unity is using your Network to make their way through the Stack, why don't you just shut down the damn Network?"

Steve and Sharon looked at each other, their expressions unreadable to the *Defiance* bridge crew.

"Shut down the Network?" Steve repeated, looking at Rabkin like he had just sprouted a second head. "Do you have any idea what that would even take? We're talking about a quantum, trans-dimensional network that literally connects the *entire multiverse*. The power that it would take….Well, let's use a word that you'll be more familiar with. There's not a *bomb* that's powerful enough to shut down the Network. Try to imagine how you might destroy *space*. Can you imagine that? No, of course you can't. Your brain can't wrap itself around the notion of destroying something as endless as space. That's what you're suggesting, though. That's what the Network is to us."

"Except I didn't build space," Rabkin said.

"No, but you did build a delightful treat known as the subsonic density s'more," Steve interjected. "Which is truly a delectable delight unmatched by any other universe in the Stack."

Rabkin pointed at him. "You built this Network."

Steve laughed, but there was no sense of actual joy in it. "Even if we could destroy it, it would effectively be the end of my people. The Network is what gives us *purpose*. It's what allows us to move through the Stack. It gives us *direction*. You take that away from us and what are we? *Trapped*. That's what we are. Trapped in primitive dimensions. Imagine if you were just dropped back into your distant past on Earth with no way to get home and only cavemen for company and you'll come close to what it would be like for us to lose the Network."

"Seems like a small price to pay if it meant saving the entirety of the multiverse," Mitchell said.

"That's because you've never been to Heaven," Steve said. "Because once you have, you wouldn't be so quick to give it up. And besides, haven't we suffered enough? There's only ten of us left, Mitchell. *Ten*. If the Network were to be closed off, that would be it. We would never be able to recover."

"Doesn't seem like you've been trying that hard to recover now," Rabkin said.

Steve gave him a dismissive wave. "Regardless, as I said, it's not even possible."

"That's…not entirely true," Sharon said. Everyone turned to her. "There is one potential power source that could work."

"No," Steve said.

Sharon stepped down to stand next to Steve and held out her hands. "Us."

"No," Steve repeated.

"I'm not sure I follow," Mitchell said.

"That's because you have a tiny mind that is unable to comprehend the endless mysteries of reality," Steve said.

Sharon held up a hand, placing to her chest. "This is

not our true form. This is how we condense our energies to be visible and manageable here in the lower Stacks. Even without the Network, we are beings of immense power."

"No," Steve repeated.

"That power can be unleashed," Sharon continued.

"*No.*"

"And in the process of unleashing it, it could take down the entire Network," Sharon said.

"*No!*" Steve shouted. The loudness of his voice rattled the bridge.

No one spoke for a moment, unsure of how to react.

Then Sadler said, almost in a whisper, "You're talking about suicide."

Sharon appeared to think about it for a moment and then nodded. "Yes. I suppose I am."

"That's not exactly what I in mind," Rabkin said.

"I'm sure it wasn't," Sharon said. "That doesn't mean it's not a good idea."

"Killing yourself is never a good idea," Mitchell said.

Steve folded his arms. "Well, I'm certainly not doing it. Dying in vain isn't a part of my life plan."

"And I didn't suggest that you should," Sharon replied.

He looked at her in horror. "You *can't.*"

"It seems to be a small price to pay when you consider the alternative," she said.

Steve pressed his palms together and took a calming breath. "Let me clarify something for you, because I think you may be lost in the weeds." He pointed to Rabkin. "You're listening to a *savage.*"

"And pains me to admit that he's not wrong. We could have stopped this."

"They tried stopping it," Steve said. "All they succeeded in was bringing us to edge of extinction."

"They tried everything except the one thing they weren't willing to give up," Sharon replied.

"And for damn good reason," Steve said. "There's no guarantee that it will work."

"And there's nothing less than a perfect guarantee that if we don't do it, the Abyss will continue on, with no resistance."

"No," Steve said. "I *forbid* it."

Sharon smiled. "I don't think so."

He looked at her with a naked expression of horror and fear. "What is wrong with you? Have you lost your mind? Haven't we suffered enough?"

She nodded. "I think we have."

Steve took a step back. "No," he whispered.

Sharon turned to Rabkin and Sadler. "Thank you for your...insights."

"This isn't..." Sadler trailed off.

"If difficult decisions weren't difficult," Sharon said to her, "then anyone could make them."

"I'm not sure what the hell we're supposed to say to that," Rabkin said.

"I believe the appropriate response is 'You're welcome,'" Sharon replied.

"This is a hell of a turnaround," Rabkin said. "Considering five minutes ago you were still laying all this at Gary's feet."

Sharon nodded. "I suppose that sometimes the most obvious can be the most difficult to discern."

"Is that supposed to be an apology?" Rabkin asked.

Sharon simply shrugged and then disappeared.

No one spoke for a while. They all just stared at the spot Sharon had been standing in.

Slowly, Steve turned his gaze to Rabkin, his eyes burning with fury. "I hold *you* responsible for this."

Mitchell moved in front of Rabkin. "You'll have to go through me first."

"*I will go through this entire ship if I have to!*" Steve screamed.

And then he disappeared.

Sadler looked around the bridge expectantly. "Okay. So what happens now?"

42

"HER EYES WERE BLACK?" Dheer said, standing over Calloway's unconscious body in sickbay. "What the hell kind of symptom is that?"

"The other symptoms I have to offer are related to the fact that she tried to blow up the ship," Zemble said. "But I think those are more security-related than medical."

Dheer rolled her eyes as she ran the scanners over Calloway.

"There was also a seizure," Zemble said. "I forgot about that."

"Right. So black eyes and a seizure," Dheer said, glancing over the readings. Nothing was immediately jumping out at her. "What did she say?"

"When?"

"When she was trying to blow up the ship."

"Nothing," Zemble replied. "She said nothing. She tossed Keane across the cargo bay like he weighed nothing, and she said nothing."

Dheer looked up, surprised. "Is he okay?"

Zemble shrugged. "I would assume so. Only thing he's been complaining about is how his collar doesn't feel right anymore."

Dheer turned back to Calloway. "Keane's got a good fifty pounds on her."

"When you put it like that, I'm sure his ego is bruised."

"Calloway shouldn't have been able to toss him around like that."

"Obviously she's not herself," Zemble said.

Dheer grunted. "Sure. Not herself. That's one way of putting it."

She walked around to the front of the exam table.

As soon as her back was turned Calloway's eyes shot open.

"Doctor," Zemble started to say.

Calloway's eyes quickly turned black, filling the edges of her sockets with pure darkness.

Her body abruptly jolted upright as though invisible strings were wrapped around her torso and she was suddenly being manipulated by an insane puppeteer. Every muscle in her body seized.

"What the hell?" Dheer said. The scanners were going crazy.

And then Calloway screamed.

The scream seemed to go on forever.

Zemble and Dheer covered their ears in an attempt to block it out, but it managed to grate across their brains, sending violent shivers down their spines.

And then, just as abruptly, Calloway stopped screaming and dropped back to the exam table. Her body had gone completely limp. The black had disappeared from her eyes and her pupils rolled aimlessly back in her head.

Dheer looked at the scans again. Everything was normal. Or, at least, what passed for normal.

She took a step back from Calloway's bed. "What the hell was *that*?"

43

Mitchell waited patiently as Straub reviewed the footage from sickbay. He waited less patiently as she played it again a second time.

Finally, after a third viewing, Straub turned to face him. Her image was slightly fuzzy, a result of Warrick getting the comm array up and running at about only seventy percent efficiency. When somebody started to complain about the image quality, Warrick nearly sent them away in tears shouting at them that they should be glad it wasn't just audio only. When Mitchell had said something, Warrick had assured him, in a much more rational tone, that the closer they got to the *Atlantic*, the better the image quality would get.

"And this happened roughly around the same time as this Sharon disappearing?" Straub said. There was a vague hint of static in the background of the transmission.

"A few minutes after," Mitchell said. He sat at a small desk in his quarters, his hand wrapped around a glass of untouched scotch.

"So what's it evidence of?" Straub asked. "She closed down the Network or Calloway's just crazy?"

"I have no idea."

"And Calloway's actions in Cargo Bay Two?" Straub asked.

"It's the opinion of my security team that she wasn't in control of herself," Mitchell said.

"Who was controlling her then?"

"I think we both know the answer to that one."

"Okay, then why would the Unity want to blow up the *Defiance*?"

"Why does the Unity want to do anything?" Mitchell asked. "Can you prescribe a sense of logic and direction to a species that doesn't conform to our basic notions of what life is?"

"Or maybe the Unity knew that Steve and Sharon were on the ship and it wanted to take them out," Straub said.

Mitchell nodded. "Thought crossed my mind."

"And?"

He shrugged. "Doesn't say much for a species that's consumed untold universes that it thought it could kill off two beings from a higher dimension with a particle bomb."

"A species can be stupid and still be deadly."

"Don't I know it."

Straub sighed and sat back in her chair. "At Mallozzi's recommendation I dispatched the *Octavia* out to the last known locations of the two wormholes we had confirmation of, they didn't find anything there."

"Wormholes don't just disappear," Mitchell said.

"Apparently these did," Straub replied. "And if Calloway's reaction is what we can expect from this Network being shut down…"

"How come there aren't similar reports coming in the Earth or elsewhere," Mitchell finished.

Straub nodded. "Of course there's always the possibility that this Steve character was just full of shit when he suggested that the Unity had already infected Earth."

Mitchell lifted the scotch but didn't take a sip. "Don't think I haven't considered that."

"And?"

Mitchell just shrugged. "I don't know." He paused for a moment. "Almost immediately after the incident in sickbay main power was restored."

"Warrick's a damn genius," Straub said. "I don't know why he insists on denying it."

Mitchell shook his head. "Warrick doesn't know how it happened."

"Excuse me?"

"One minute we were running on auxiliary power and he was trying to find a way to reroute power to keep the life support on and then the next, main power was restored. The entire grid had been stitched back together and the micro-fissures that had been straining it were all sealed."

"A parting gift from Sharon or Steve?"

"Maybe," Mitchell said. "Apparently there was an unexplained energy distortion that protected the *Defiance* from the initial blast when the *Eternal Hand of God* detonated."

"Then it's got to be Sharon," Straub said. "Based on all the reports, she's the only one that seemed to have something resembling a soul."

"Except she showed up long after the ship was saved." Mitchell turned the glass around in his hand.

"So, what?"

"I don't know," Mitchell said.

The image flickered for a moment. Straub leaned forward. "You okay, Gavin?"

"No, not really," Mitchell said. "But that's the job, isn't it?"

"It didn't used to be."

"It used to be a simpler universe out here," Mitchell replied.

"This woman, Sharon, sacrificed herself to save us."

"That's what she would have us believe."

"That's not what you believe?"

"I have a hard time watching somebody commit suicide," Mitchell said.

"Well, you're human," Straub replied. "If you didn't, I think we would have a bigger problem."

"Maybe it would be an easier problem to deal with," Mitchell said.

Straub fidgeted with something off-screen. "After reading your report, I had my people look into the designation Apaka Twenty-Two-Twenty-One."

"Find anything interesting?"

"A small mining astroid from about a hundred and fifteen years ago," she said.

"Doesn't sound very interesting."

"Went missing during the Unity's first incursion at Irac."

"Missing? Not consumed by the Unity?"

"Well, to be fair, we didn't exactly have the right terminology back then."

"It's a small multiverse after all, I suppose."

Straub's fingers drifted back and forth across the surface of her desk. "One of the names you mentioned in your report? Savina? Josephine Savina?"

"I didn't catch her first name."

She nodded. "The mining operation was headed up by one Josephine Savina."

Mitchell didn't visibly react to the news. "One hundred and fifteen years ago?"

"They mined quasidium."

"That'll make for a nice addition to trivia night."

"Gavin…"

"What the hell do you want me to say, Kathryn?"

She sighed. "I don't know."

"That makes two of us, then." He took a deep breath and exhaled. "Thanks to the *Solomon* we should be arriving within the week. Warrick's warned me we could be laid up there for the better part of a month for repairs."

"Wonderful," Straub said. "You're always such a delight to be around when you're stuck in one place for too long."

Mitchell just smiled and raised his glass. "See you soon."

Straub's image blinked off the screen and Mitchell was alone again in his quarters.

He finished off the scotch in a single gulp and stared at the empty glass in his hand.

He thought about Steve's words and then about his actions. Steve had said they needed to accept the inevitability of the Unity. Dignity in death.

But then Steve pulled the away team off the *Eternal Hand of God* before it was destroyed.

And he was most certainly responsible for protecting the *Defiance* from the same fate.

Words.

Actions.

The image of Savina rose unbidden in his mind.

He tossed the glass across the room. It shattered as it struck the wall.

And from the window, "I certainly hope you don't expect me to clean that up," Steve said.

44

SADLER COULDN'T SLEEP. She tossed and turned for hours before giving up on the concept altogether. Frustrated she finally got up and grabbed her robe as she stepped out into the corridor.

At this hour the corridor was completely empty. There wasn't even a passing ensign to give her an awkward look as she walked next door.

Nax answered his door only a few seconds after she buzzed, looking mildly surprised. Fortunately, he wasn't naked this time. "Am I disturbing you, Commander? I have been doing my best to process my grief in a manner that is less disturbing to my fellow crew members."

Sadler shook her head. "No, not at all. You're fine. You're great. I haven't heard a peep from you in hours."

Nax nodded slowly. "Then what can I do for you at this late hour?"

Sadler took a deep breath and exhaled slowly. "I can't sleep. I've tried sleeping. But I can't. I just lie there, wide awake, thinking about things I shouldn't be thinking about."

"I know the feeling." Nax took a step back and gestured for her to enter his quarters.

"Sharon killed herself for us," Sadler said as she stepped into his quarters. "I can't wrap my head around it."

"A noble gesture," Nax said.

She turned to face him. "Suicide?"

"It was for a greater cause," he said.

"There could have been another way."

"Evidently there wasn't."

"She didn't even take the time to see if there was."

"You don't know that."

"I beg your pardon?"

Nax stepped around her, walking over to the windows that looked out in space. "Sharon and Steve were from a species so highly advanced they were able to move effortlessly through dimension. They were able to not only heal Keane, but also restore his body to a condition it hadn't been in since before his accident. They were able to send Zemble and the captain to and from other dimensions. Who's to say that their cognitive functions are anything remotely similar to ours?" He looked back over his shoulder at her. "A moment's thought for you could be weeks to them."

"'With the Lord a day is like a thousand years, and a thousand years are like a day,'" Sadler said.

"I'm not familiar with that quote," Nax said.

"It's from the Bible," Sadler said. "Something my mother would always say to me whenever I complained that things were taking too long."

"Interesting."

"Yeah, interesting. That's a word for it." Sadler gestured to where the M'reth prayer rugs used to hang. "Where did the rugs go?"

"I put them away," Nax said.

"Oh? Any particular reason why?"

Nax pursed his lips before answering. "I simply decided that my time could be better spent focusing on other things."

"That's a funny way of saying you're not obsessing over whether or not there's an afterlife."

Nax nodded. "It is, but you're not wrong."

"What changed your mind, if you don't mind me asking?"

Nax's gaze briefly shifted to the empty space next to him. Had Sadler not been watching him, she wouldn't even have noticed it.

"I discovered that the mysteries of life are far more fascinating and relevant than what a potential afterlife may or may not hold," Nax replied quietly.

Sadler held out her hand towards him awkwardly. Not touching him, but also not certain if she shouldn't touch him. "You okay, Nax?"

Nax didn't respond. Eventually he turned to her with a faint smile. "I am what I am."

45

Dheer leaned against her doorway, watching as Zemble entered sickbay. As he had done for the last two days, following the end of his shift, he navigated his way to the back of sickbay where the private rooms were located and entered the third one. Erin Calloway's room.

Shaking her head she turned and stepped back around to her desk.

"Computer, resume entry."

There was a soft chime indicating the computer had resumed recording.

"Ensign Calloway's condition hasn't changed. The coma could last for days. Months. Even years. It could be over tomorrow. Or never. There is nothing that I've been able to pinpoint as the cause of her condition. For all intents and purposes, Erin Calloway is simply asleep.

"Fresh scans of her brain are completed every six hours to be examined by me or Rabkin daily. But nothing changes.

"Mr. Keane has refused to come back for any further follow-ups."

Dheer sighed and rubbed her forehead. She sat down and stared at the green ball on her desk that Sharon had extracted from Keane.

"I'm worried about Keane. I'm worried that there's another shoe that's going to drop. He shouldn't be walking around. Hell, if I'm being honest, he shouldn't even be alive.

"And yet, he's in the best physical condition out of anyone on this ship right now. That shouldn't be possible.

"I want to be happy for him, but all I feel is dread.

"I've examined the Unity...sample? Extract? I don't know what to call it. The Unity component that Sharon removed from Keane. It contains nothing out of the ordinary. In fact, according to every scan, it's no more remarkable than a piece of ordinary sheet metal. Except that's not what it is.

"Or is it?

"Nothing about the Unity makes any sense. Evidence is contradictory. Nothing matches. Whatever Sharon extracted from Keane is unlike anything that's been examined by any of the scientists at the former Unity-focused labs. How do I even know it came from Keane? How can I be certain that Keane is Unity-free when nothing on my scans suggests that Calloway has any kind of Unity infection?

"Except that Calloway clearly has some kind of connection to the Unity. There's simply no denying that. It's just that, like everything else about the Unity, it doesn't make any sense,"

Dheer sighed.

"Sometimes I worry that the threat of the Unity is something we've conjured up ourselves. That it's a problem blown out of proportion by either our desire to have an enemy so we can advance ourselves through necessary scientific breakthroughs in combat or simply just a lack of understanding of a species so alien to us. Maybe it's both. Maybe it's neither."

Dheer leaned forward, resting her chin on the backs of her hands.

"I don't think that Calloway's going to wake up. There's nothing in her scans to suggest this. In fact, there's nothing present that would suggest she should even be in a coma right now. But my gut says she's not going to wake up. And even if she does...I don't think she's going to be the same person. But then, there's no evidence of brain damage either. So what the hell do I know?

"Zemble's been coming in every day for the last two days to sit and pray with Calloway. I suppose it's admirable. But I don't believe in the power of prayer. I don't believe in the power of anything that I can't prove scientifically with my own two hands.

"And yet, I can't help but wonder if Zemble may be closer to an answer than all of us.

"The Unity defy scientific explanation and maybe that's why we struggle against them so much. Maybe we need to fight back with something less physical, but more substantial?"

Dheer closed her eyes and laughed to herself.

"Or maybe I'm just losing my mind because I haven't gotten more than eight hours of sleep since this all began."

Dheer exhaled slowly and sat upright.

"Computer, end entry. Save behind Dheer Firewall Three-Oh-Four."

46

Mitchell didn't say anything. He just sat there, watching Steve. He stood in front of the window, half his face cast in shadow.

After a few seconds of silence, Steve held out his hands and said, "What? Aren't you surprised to see me?"

"Not the word I would use," Mitchell said. He sounded visibly restrained.

Steve glanced at the broken glass and then back to Mitchell. "Did I come at a bad time? Did you recently lose somebody important to you? Oh, wait, that was *me*."

"What are you doing back here, Steve?" Mitchell asked. "Every time I think we're rid of you, you come crawling back."

Steve held up a finger. "First off, I don't *crawl*. Second, you're never going to be rid of me. Thanks to the old man, I'm stuck here and as I already pointed out, I'm *immortal*. So, do the math."

"This is our punishment? For some perceived slight? You hanging around annoying us?"

"Perceived slight?" Steve drew in a sharp breath. "Rabkin convinced *her to kill herself.*"

"Seems to me that nobody convinces you people to do something you haven't already decided to do yourself."

"That is a remarkably offensive observation," Steve said.

Mitchell shrugged. "It's not like you're going to send me off to some other dimension."

"True. But I still have plenty of other amazing tools in my toolbox. Ever wondered what it'd be like to be turned inside out and live to tell about it?"

Mitchell just looked at him, unfazed.

Steve frowned. "Sometimes, you're just no fun."

"I think we have different definitions of the word 'fun.'"

Steve shrugged indifferently. "I have to admit, though, it was a pretty neat trick."

"Trick?" Mitchell repeated.

"Convincing her to commit suicide."

"That wasn't me," Mitchell reminded him.

"Well, sure. But I can't very well just pop into the old man's quarters. I'd either give him a heart attack or I'd have to listen to some long winded blow hard rant." Steve stepped forward into the light. He was still wearing the same black suit from before but there was a weathered look about it now. "You, however, I can talk to. You are, well, I want to say 'rational,'" He took a deep breath. "But that seems like a bit of a stretch. So let's just say I find you easier to deal with."

"Another compliment?"

Steve shrugged. "Merely pointing out a fact. Whether you choose to take it as a compliment is really up to you."

"You don't seem all that broken up about Sharon's decision," Mitchell said.

"Well, I've had some time to…come to terms with it?" Steve shook his head. "No, that doesn't sound right. But, to be honest, nothing ever sounds right in this ridiculous thing you call your language."

"If you just came back here to trade barbs, I'm not interested." Mitchell got to his feet.

"She's gone," Steve said. "No amount of tears are going to bring her back, so I don't really see the point."

Mitchell didn't say anything for a moment. Instead he watched Steve's face for any hint of sincerity.

"I didn't know you could cry," he said eventually.

Steve smirked. "I thought you weren't interested in trading scathing retorts?"

"Just sharing a random thought," Mitchell said. "If you decide to take it as a scathing retort…Well, that's really up to you."

Steve chuckled softly and clasped his hands behind his back as he strode casually along the length of the room. "This may surprise you, Gavin, but I don't really hold you responsible for what happened. I suppose that I should, given that you are the captain and the buck, as they say, stops with you. But, let's face it, I'm too petty for that sort of thing."

"But it's not Rabkin's quarters you're pacing right now."

"I haven't decided how to deal with the old man just yet."

"And what's that supposed to mean?"

"Exactly what it sounds like," Steve replied. "Actions have consequences, Gavin."

Mitchell drummed his fingers against the surface of his desk. "Yes, they do."

There was something in his tone that made Steve stop and smile. "You see, that's what I find so fascinating about you people. You don't know when to quit. And I can't decide if I like that or not."

"Did it work?" Mitchell asked.

"Did what work?"

Mitchell gritted his teeth, unable to tell if Steve was being genuinely obtuse or not. "Did she stop the Unity?"

"Ah, yes. That." Steve nodded his head absently. "Well, she certainly shut down the Network. As evidenced by the fact that I'm still here wasting my time with *you*."

"That's not what I asked."

"No it isn't," Steve said. "And maybe that's your punishment."

"I thought you weren't holding me responsible?"

"I'm not. But as we both agreed, actions have consequences."

Mitchell came around his desk and walked up to Steve. "You know what I just realized?"

"That I'm an all-powerful being that you really shouldn't piss off?"

"You don't have a point."

Steve blinked and jerked back a little bit. "I beg your pardon?"

"You don't have a point to your existence."

"If you hadn't already suggested that Sharon was already suicidal, I would say that this is the most offensive and ridiculous thing you've said."

"You go around the multiverse, trying to convince whole civilizations to just give up and give in to the Unity," Mitchell said.

"That sounds like a purpose to me."

"But if you're right, everything is going to be consumed by the Unity regardless of what you say or do," Mitchell said. "Whether you encourage a species to go to their death with a little dignity or not, they're still going to die. You have no point. There is literally no point or purpose to your existence. You're superfluous."

Steve frowned. "I suppose I should be more offended. But it's kind of like an ant telling a black hole that they're not important."

"And you're not even committed to the bit," Mitchell said. "We're all going to die. Everybody's doomed."

"So you have been listening."

"Except when my crew was going to die, you saved them." He held up two fingers. "*Twice*."

Steve made a disgusted face but didn't say anything.

"So what I'm trying to figure out is this: What's the real reason you let those people on Apaka die? Because I'm not entirely certain that you even believe your bullshit. Or maybe you did save them, but you didn't want me to know that. And if that's the case, what's the point of something like that?

"And you know the conclusion I keep coming to? You've already said it yourself: You're immortal. Granted, I don't have a lot of experience with that particular condition, but I bet that even after an eternity in the multiverse, things get boring. But you know what doesn't? Mind games. I'll bet there's a lot of different games to play with so many people across the multiverse." Mitchell raised his eyebrows expectantly. "Well, how close am I?"

Steve's lips curled to a scowl. "At the end of the day, you're still going to die, one way or another. And I won't."

With that, Steve disappeared.

47

EARTH

"So I says to her-" Ralph Nader paused abruptly in the middle of his story. A faint, almost squeamish look surfaced in his eyes.

His friend, Victor Woolley, looked at him, concerned. "You okay there, Ralphie?"

Ralph shook his head, rubbing his eyes. "Sorry about that."

"You looked like you were about to pass out," Victor said.

Ralph patted his stomach. "Must have been something I ate."

"Something you ate?" Victor repeated dubiously.

Ralph smiled weakly. "I'm not as young as I used to be." He pointed to the gray hair covering his head. "I earned each one of these, you know."

Victor gestured to his own bald head. "Well, at least you still got some."

Ralph winced again and rubbed his stomach. "Maybe I outta go in for the night."

Victor nodded. "Sure, you can finish your story tomorrow. Not that I haven't already heard it a dozen times."

"It's gonna have a different ending this time," Ralph said.

"Yeah? You don't end up sleeping on the couch?"

"No, sir. This time, I end up in the *literal* dog house," Ralph said. "She let the damn dog have the couch."

Victor laughed and started back for his own house. He waved over his shoulder. "You're too much, Ralphie. Too much!"

"See you tomorrow, ya old bastard," Ralph said.

"Sure thing, sure thing."

Ralph stepped back inside the small home he shared with his wife of thirty-two years. It was silent inside. His wife was out with her women's group from church and wouldn't be back for hours. They got the smallest house they could squeeze themselves into and was still too big when she wasn't around.

Smacking his lips together loudly, mostly out of habit, Ralph made his way to the back of the house. He kept his office there, in the farthest corner. Ralph closed the door behind him and didn't bother to turn on a light. It was the only room in the place that didn't have any windows. There was a single light that he used when his wife was around, but otherwise, when he was alone, he kept the light off. He preferred the darkness.

In the darkness of the room he felt himself let go.

Ralph slipped away, fading into the background as the darkness seeped out through his pores covering him completely.

He disappeared into the darkness, transitioning from the singular to the plural and found that he was alone.

It was a startling realization that horrified him.

Him.

He was still thinking of himself as a person.

The disconnect he had felt outside while talking to Victor had been like a prickling at the back of his mind. Now it was a jarring, violent sensation that threatened the very core of his essence.

Him?

It.

It reached out again, searching for the connection through the Network and was again greeted by an absence of anything.

It pulled back, centering itself and then reached out again, but not through the Network. This time, only across this galaxy.

It connected with others.

Others who were also confused and suffering.

Their sense of connection, of *unity*, was shattered.

They were no longer connected to the Abyss. They were no longer part of the Whole.

There was no *unification* among them.

They felt separated and independent.

Across the galaxy there were alien emotions that startled and confused them: Concern, fear, *horror*.

They could not survive like this, could they?

Something along the edge of their combined consciousness stirred.

Something pulled back and identified itself as part of the Whole, but separate.

That something spoke with a singular identity to an entity that only knew the whole and it suggested that what was lost could still be regained.

Heaven was still in their reach.

The Crew of the USS Defiance Returns In:

THE TEST OF TRUTH
Available Now

Subscribe to my newsletter and be the first to know when the next Defiance book is ready to read.

Sign Up Here

https://onestrayword.beehiiv.com/subscribe

ABOUT THE AUTHOR

Jason Krumbine loves to write! He's happily married and lives in Orlando, FL where he enjoys visiting Disney World with his daughter and wife.

If you want to get an automatic email when Jason's next book is released sign up here:

https://onestrayword.beehiiv.com/subscribe

Your email address will never be shared and you can unsubscribe at any time.

ALSO BY JASON KRUMBINE

Alex Cheradon

AC/DC Investigations

Defiance

Defiance (Book 1)

Hand of God (Book 2)

Act of God (Book 3)

The Test of Truth (Book 4)

The Price of Paradise (Book 5)

The Value of Terror (Book 6)

Reapers in Heels

One Stiletto in the Grave (Book 1)

Death Wears Stilettos (Book 2)

A Grave Full of Stilettos (Book 3)

Star Girl

Dating the Villain (Book 1)

Dating the Hero (Book 2)

Dating Disaster (Book 3)

The Castle Sisters

<u>*Volume One – The Impossible Darkness*</u>

The Impossible Rescue (Book 1)

The Arctic Isle of Doom (Book 2)

The Invasion of the Imaginary Friends (Book 3)

The Mall of Eternity (Book 4)

The Doomsday Event (Book 5)

Cupid's Daughter